For Butch
Merry Christmas
1994
love
Joe & Elepe

CAMARO CITY

ALAN STERNBERG

CAMARO CITY

HARCOURT
BRACE &
COMPANY

NEW YORK
SAN DIEGO
LONDON

Requests to make copies of any part of the
work should be mailed to: Harcourt Brace & Company,
6277 Sea Harbor Drive, Orlando, Florida 32887-6777.

Grateful acknowledgment is made to
The New Yorker, where "Blazer," "Moose,"
"Camaro City," "Bilt-Rite," and "Hober" first appeared, in
slightly different form. "Broken Violin" first appeared in *Yankee,*
and "Splat," also in slightly different form, in *Northeast,*
the Sunday magazine of *The Hartford Courant.*

The author would also like to thank Roger Angell.

Library of Congress Cataloging-in-Publication Data
Sternberg, Alan.
Camaro City / Alan Sternberg.—1st ed.
p.   cm.
ISBN 0-15-115373-6
1. City and town life—Connecticut—Fiction.
2. Working class—Connecticut—Fiction.
3. Unemployed—Connecticut—Fiction
I. Title.
PS3569.T417C36   1994
813'.54—dc20 94-5118

The text was set in Bembo.

Designed by Linda Lockowitz
Printed in the United States of America
First edition

A B C D E

*For my parents
and grandmother*

Contents

CAMARO CITY

BLAZER

SWEET LIFE TRUCKS came and went constantly on the interstate behind the high school, bearing groceries to far-flung supermarkets. The trucks were yellow and had different inspirational messages on their sides, and the students, perennially bored, had begun to keep track of them: "A CHILD IS A GIFT FROM GOD!" "TO HAVE A FRIEND—YOU MUST BE ONE!" "WE ARE ALL BROTHERS AND SISTERS!"

The first odd thing to happen on this Saturday night was that a Sweet Life truck stopped at Burger King. The bunch who spent a lot of time hanging around in the parking lot had never seen that before. "HUG A SENIOR CITIZEN TODAY!" the truck proclaimed, and Rudy D'Angelo, who was beside the Dumpster, stiff-armed Jeff Fontaine in the shoulder and yelled, "Hey! This truck's for you!" He waved his arms. "Jeff'll hug her tonight! He'll hug her tonight!"

It got a few laughs. There were about twenty juniors and seniors gathered around their cars and pickup

1

trucks. After a while, the Sweet Life driver returned with his hamburger and climbed into the cab and then the truck moved off slowly—a yellow curtain withdrawing to reveal a panorama of traprock and sumac bushes behind the restaurant. Beyond the blacktop, a steep bank descended to a neighborhood of small ranch houses. The bizarre, shaggy objects over there were sections of trees that happened to catch the full blast of the street lamps. Farther off were the headlights on Interstate 91.

"Just shut up," Jeff said to Rudy. Jeff was having an affair with a second-grade teacher—theoretically a secret, although the news had gotten around pretty fast. Rudy even knew the teacher's name: Veronica Pinsky.

In a moment Rudy was bellowing over the sumac bushes. "She don't love me, she just loves Darryl Strawb'ry," he sang, to the tune of the ZZ Top song "She Don't Love Me, She Loves My Automobile." This was a reference to his own girlfriend, Diane, who had the usual number of defects, and not to Jeff's, who was in her mid-twenties and perfect enough, in Rudy's opinion, to be noticed by rock stars. Diane wasn't around tonight, because she and Rudy had had a fight.

Jeff was a friend from the baseball team. He was probably the best high-school pitcher in Connecticut; he hadn't lost a game in two years. He would be going to Wesleyan in the fall. Rudy, a junior, pitched only in relief—in fact, he pitched only when the team was a long way behind. He tended to give up a lot of line drives.

The song was also because Rudy and Jeff and Mark Spaginsky had gone to the ZZ Top concert Thursday night at the New Haven Coliseum. Spaginsky was the only one who had liked the show. He wasn't so much a friend as someone Rudy tolerated. Most of Rudy's friends were looking for summer jobs, but Spaginsky was facing the prospect of a month at a computer-adventure camp and was fighting with his parents to get out of it.

"You're acting like a jerk," Spaginsky told Rudy now.

"I don't take shit from you!" Rudy said, genuinely angry. "You *belong* in computer-adventure camp, you stupid yuppie."

There had been a big crowd at Paul Bacewicz's funeral a month earlier—anyone who had a motorcycle had ridden it to the mortuary and from there to the church. The priest seemed upset. The newspaper ran an editorial about failure to learn from tragedy. Bacewicz had died when his Kawasaki Ninja hit a parked car on a narrow neighborhood street. The police claimed he was going fifty miles per hour and had his front wheel off the ground. No one at the high school was surprised about that; it was the way Bacewicz often drove. The accident didn't discourage anyone from riding motorcycles. In fact, a few of the kids who didn't have motorcycles went out and bought them afterward, and some of Bacewicz's classmates put bumper stickers on their cars exhorting drivers to watch out for motorcyclists. Bacewicz had been the third casualty since the start of the year, if you counted the snowmobile accident back in February, in which Bobby Hurteau was killed. There had also been Doug Goldberg's broken leg in a motor-cycle wreck in April. Now it was early June. There were three weeks of school left.

Rudy used to have a Honda with red flames painted on the gas tank—one of the old 750 four-cylinders. He'd rarely lifted the front wheel. It bothered him that he was so cautious with it—it scared him even to see telephone poles going by. After Bacewicz died, his mother shrieked whenever he tried to take it out of the garage, and finally he sold it. Now all he did at night was hang around at Burger King or, if he was with Di-ane, stay home and watch the Mets. The night before their fight, they had watched at Rudy's house—the Mets at the Astros. "He's old," Diane said at one point. "He's going bald." She meant Nolan Ryan. "Flame-thrower," the announcer said.

Diane went to St. Catherine's. When she was younger and at a different parochial school, she had once won the citywide spelling bee.

"He's already struck out Strawberry twice," Rudy said.

"Poor Darryl," Diane said. She tended to shift to baby talk when she mentioned Strawberry. She acted as if Strawberry needed to be cuddled. Rudy reached out with his big toe and punched a different channel button on the cable box, which was on the coffee table next to his father's ashtray, a ceramic Budweiser beer wagon. The screen erupted into smoke and flames, and laser beams shot into a woman's bodice. Rudy didn't recog-nize the music, but he liked it.

"How come you never baby-talk when you talk

about me?" he said. "How come you never act like I need to be cuddled?"

"Because you're too sarcastic."

The Mets won the game, it turned out, and Diane left fairly early, although it was Friday. The next morning, the two of them went to the regional Special Olympics, which were being held at the Choate Rosemary Hall prep school, five miles away in Wallingford. Diane had to go because she and five other members of the St. Catherine's track team had volunteered to oversee the croquet and horseshoe-pitching events. They all wore makeup with their green sweatsuits and shiny green team jackets. Rudy went along to hang around. Groups of retarded athletes—mostly kids, but with a few adults mixed in—marched around the track behind the Governor's Foot Guard, a collection of elderly men wearing garish red coats and hats that resembled giant Q-Tips. The mayor gave a speech from the reviewing stand. A number of girls from the prep school wandered over from their dormitories to help with the cheering and hugging. They wore baggy sweatshirts and loose, pastel-colored shorts, and they looked sleepy. Several had hair that was still wet from their morning showers. Men from Kiwanis and Civitan were running other events—the wheelchair races and the hundred-yard walk. Rudy noticed a few of his father's friends among them. They had knit shirts that stretched over their bellies and they smoked when they thought no one was looking. Some of the athletes asked for cigarettes, and then a counsellor complained because two members of her team had done the hundred-yard walk while holding cigarettes. Rudy saw George Angiletta, one of the Civitan officials, apologizing about this. He shrugged his shoulders and lifted his arms dramatically.

At the awards stand, a girl wearing a sash that said "Miss So. Central Conn." was handing out ribbons. She had broad cheekbones and blue eyeshadow, and wore a tight pink jumpsuit. Her long hair was bushed out in a mass of elaborate curls, and white athletic socks sprouted from her sneakers and covered the calves of the jumpsuit. Rudy saw the Choate Rosemary Hall girls exchanging glances behind her back. "There's a Miss South Central Connecticut," he heard one of them say.

"She looks more like Miss Pepto-Bismol," another one said, staring at the pink jumpsuit.

"That stinks," Diane said later, when Rudy told her about it. They were driving home in Diane's father's car. "Who do they think they are?"

"What're you worried about? She didn't hear them."

"They were probably making fun of us, too."

"They were not."

Rudy thought of something. "Did you ever think of doing that? Any of that beauty-contest stuff?"

Diane was driving. Rudy watched the fire hydrants and parked pickup trucks zip by. They were in his neighborhood, between the Burger King Plaza and I-91. There were small religious statues on several of the side lawns, and there were fibreglass Macho canopies on the backs of some of the pickups. Blazers and Broncos were parked everywhere, rising over huge, crenellated tires. Their underskeletons and mechanical genitalia were proudly exposed, and the doors were so high that it seemed you'd need ladders to get into them.

"One thing about the girls around here," Rudy said. "When they get dressed up, they put on the dog. I mean, she was sort of asking for it."

Diane was staring through the windshield. She seemed angry.

"You can be Miss Northeast Greater Solar System if you want," Rudy said, "but let me know ahead of time so I can prepare myself for the embarrassment."

"Shut up."

Diane stopped in front of his house.

"I guess this means I don't get a kiss," Rudy said.

"She's out there kissing retarded people, and people are making fun of her," Diane said. "What's so great about you? You just want to pitch an inning without giving up five runs, right?"

"Don't tell me to shut up. I never tell you to shut up."

"You were talking about how her makeup was thick enough to stop bullets."

"I didn't say that, *they* said that. Don't get me mixed up with any prep-school girls."

"Sure, but it's exactly the kind of thing you'd say," Diane said. "You think you have some special privilege where you can be critical all the time."

Rudy got out and shut the door and looked back through the window. Diane was wearing red fingernail polish—her hands were on the steering wheel and the polish made them look lethal.

"That's like the meanest thing you can do," she

said. "Make fun of somebody's clothes. Make fun of somebody's makeup."

She drove away without looking at him.

"Burger King is closed, Spags," Rudy said. "Jester's Courtyard is closed. You should've gone home with the thirteen-year-olds. You should've gone home to listen to ZZ Top and play air guitar in front of the mirror."

It was almost midnight, but the high-school kids were still scattered around the blacktop. Car doors were open and radios and cassette players were blasting. Saturday nights often passed this way. Spaginsky lit a cigarette. "I don't care what you say," he told Rudy. "Some of their early songs were good. 'La Grange' was good."

"That was before they decided they could make a lot of money off morons like you."

Something was wrong with Jeff's father's Blazer. It smelled like gasoline, and Jeff had parked it under a light in a corner of the lot and had the hood up. Even if Jeff could fix it, he wouldn't be going home, Rudy knew— he'd be going to visit the second-grade teacher. Rudy lived almost across the street from Jeff, but he'd have to get a ride from someone else.

"If this stupid thing's broken, Spags, my father's going to kill me," Jeff said from under the hood. "Maybe I should run away to computer-adventure camp with you. I'd rather be a total jerk than be dead."

"Keep talking about the stupid camp," Spaginsky said. "The first fifty times it was funny."

"You're going to Wesleyan, big shot," Rudy said

to Jeff. "That's like a four-year computer-adventure camp."

"How do you know I'm going?" Jeff said. "I could still change my mind about it."

"Oh , right," Rudy said. "That's the best thing that ever happened to you."

Police were in the bank parking lot across the street—two cruisers with their lights on, side by side but facing in opposite directions so the cops could talk to each other window to window. The cars bristled with antennas and flashers and insignia. Over here there were Blazers and Broncos and pickup trucks. Jeff's father's Blazer had flat black paint and tires that might have gone on a moon vehicle. It was parked next to Spaginsky's father's Camry, and looked to Rudy as if it were about to crawl over the Camry and chew on it.

Jeff had WPLR on the radio. When "Born in the U.S.A." came on, he emerged from beneath the hood and ran to the door. He hopped onto the metal step his father had welded below the doorframe and reached past the steering wheel to turn up the volume. The song wasn't played that much anymore. Everywhere in the lot, radios were bringing it in.

Later on, Rudy thought of how it looked: Sara Angiletta in a jean skirt and white blouse, standing in front of Dave McCauley's Suzuki Samurai with her fist in the air, lighters flicking on here and there and being held up like torches, and the Burger King sign extinguished in the background. It was like some kind of religious ceremony; it was the way it had felt a couple of years ago, back when the song was played all the time. In the concert video, Springsteen raises his fist during the chorus, and that was what Sara was doing now. The next time the chorus came around, everyone did it. Spaginsky flicked on his lighter. He and Jeff were leaning against each other, pantomiming the way Springsteen and Nils Lofgren often played their guitars together. Jeff flicked his lighter and there was a burst of light and a hot rush of air. The lighter shot upward and made a streak over the parking lot.

After the ambulance left, there was a lot of self-important standing around in groups with hands on hips by the parking-lot regulars. There was also a lot of coming and going in cars by casual acquaintances and complete strangers. Traffic usually wasn't this heavy after closing, but word had gotten out that something had happened.

"It was like the Bud Light commercial," Spaginsky said to Rudy and Sara. "The one where the space-ships come right out of the video game and they're flying around the room and the actor's shooting them with his fingers. Jeff's lucky the Blazer didn't burn up, too."

"Those cops were pretty nice about it, except for that one guy," Sara said. "He's like, 'So this is when you're not crashing motorcycles,' and I'm like, 'It's not funny.' "

Earlier, the police had cleared out the lot, but the high-school kids were used to being routed from Burger King. Once the cruisers were gone, they were back in a matter of minutes.

Rudy went off to the hospital to see Jeff, returned to report, then went back to the hospital. Dave McCauley drove him.

"I don't want to go to Wesleyan," Jeff announced suddenly when Rudy had found him the second time. He was sitting on an examining table in the emergency room, and he had been sedated. He was sniffling. He was going to stay the night, he said, but the doctor wanted to talk to his parents before admitting him. "Things are just too weird," he said.

"You're just not feeling too good right now."

"I was supposed to see what's-her-name. Veronica. I was supposed to go over there."

"You want me to tell her you can't make it?" Rudy asked.

"I can't handle this shit," Jeff said. "I'm always supposed to be doing stuff."

"You don't have to see her."

"Why'm I supposed to be smarter all the time? Why'm I supposed to strike people out all the time?"

Rudy watched as Jeff looked at his hands and then moved them around cautiously. The fingers and the bottom knuckles were covered with antibiotic cream and clear bandages. The skin looked white and flaked in places. Everyone in the parking lot had seen his hands flame up and then go out. The whole thing had happened before he'd landed on the blacktop; they'd popped blue and yellow, like flashbulbs. When the lighter jumped from his hand, he'd reached up without thinking and the other hand had caught.

"What's-her-name," he said now. "She sort of . . .

She hugs me a lot. She's nice and everything, but there's a lot of pressure."

Jeff's mother was a fifth-grade teacher at St. Martin's, and Rudy knew that Jeff got a lot of pressure from her, too. That was the reason he got good grades—not the standard thing in the neighborhood. She kept after him. She and Veronica Pinsky taught at the same school, and Jeff had told Rudy that his mother had even introduced him to Veronica. His mother didn't know this was going on. Sometimes Veronica came to the high-school games. She was red-haired and Rudy tended to stare at her from his spot on the bench. Sometimes she wore miniskirts and when she shifted position he could see her underpants.

The emergency-room doctor returned and said he couldn't reach Jeff's parents. He explained that gasoline burned at a very high temperature. Luckily, most of it had evaporated from Jeff's fingers before the explosion. It was really the vapor rising from his hands that went off. There were scattered first- and second-degree burns. He probably wouldn't need skin grafting. The doctor went off to arrange about admitting Jeff.

"I don't even know if it was mine that did it or not," Jeff said. "How could the flame go *down?* It might have been Spags' lighter."

"I sort of think you should go to sleep," Rudy said. "Take a nap or something until they bring you upstairs."

"Bruce Springsteen is pissed."

"What?"

"He doesn't like guys who go to Wesleyan."

12

"What are you talking about?"

Jeff looked around uncertainly.

"Where're your parents?" Rudy asked him.

"My father'll be pissed. I broke the Blazer. He's so crazy that one night a guy scratched it at the Moose Club and he got into a fight, and after that they wanted to kick him out of the Moose Club."

"I sort of think you should go to sleep."

"This hurts," Jeff said.

In the hospital parking lot, Rudy got back into Dave McCauley's car and they drove down Main Street and out onto I-91. There was a Sweet Life truck in the next lane. Rudy had his eyes closed and didn't see it for a minute. The frame of the window was cool and felt good against his face. Then he looked up. This truck said "Never Go to Bed Angry with Each Other!"

"Do you believe something like that happened and he wasn't even killed?" he said to Dave McCauley. "I'll tell you one thing. You and me are normal compared to a lot of people around here."

Dave said, "You're normal except for your mouth."

"Jesus," Rudy said.

There wasn't much traffic on the highway. They went over a bridge and past a flashing Mobil sign and then Rudy asked Dave to drop him off at Diane's house. When he got there, he bounced pennies off her window until she came down in her bathrobe and let him in. They went to the kitchen and Rudy told her about Jeff.

"This is just another one of those deals where you

guys run around trying to get into disasters and then one really happens and you act like it's a big surprise," Diane said. "But it's no surprise—it's just stupid."

"Nobody was trying to get into any disaster," Rudy said.

"I can't believe you thought you could come over here in the middle of the night because of something you saw on a truck."

"Well, it was because of Jeff, too," Rudy said.

Finally, Diane got dressed and drove him back to Burger King. Her parents were angry, because it was so late. Rudy really needed a ride home, but Diane's father wouldn't let her drive him that far.

"Listen," she said in the car, "I'm not that good-looking, O.K.? I know it, so you don't have to bring it up. You don't have to talk about beauty pageants. It's not a good joke, because it's not funny. I sort of think you need a different kind of girlfriend. I'm sort of surprised we even go out, except you're not that much of a big shot, either."

"That's what's driving me nuts," Rudy said vehemently. He punched the roof of the car.

"You O.K.?" Diane asked after a minute. She turned into the lot and parked and began to fool with the car's light switch. She looked at him, then twisted the dial to Off. Rudy was facing the other way. "Whenever I have a crisis it's not as big as the crisis you're having," she said.

"Your best friend didn't just blow his hands up," Rudy said. He seemed to be crying. Diane wasn't sure.

"I want to be able to impress people," he said. "I

want to be the sort of person that impresses people. That's pretty stupid and everything, but that's what I want."

Diane tilted her head back and stared at the car ceiling.

"I feel like I'm going to do something crazy," Rudy went on. "I'm sort of a baseball player. I'm sort of this, sort of that. I get jealous of people who can really do stuff. He's a good pitcher. He wasn't even that bad at the hospital, and he was drugged up."

"What're you saying? You want to burn your fingers?"

"I'm sorry he was hurt. You should have seen it. It was amazing. It was like MTV or something. If that happened to me I'd be dead. If that happened to me I'd be screaming my head off."

"Is that true about him and the teacher? I heard about that."

"Everything I'm telling you is the truth."

Diane was rotating the cone on the dash that controlled the windshield wipers. The keys were in her lap and the wipers weren't doing anything. Finally she said, "Well, maybe if you're such a chicken and such an average person that nobody admires you or anything, then maybe you won't have any disasters. You won't end up like Bacewicz or get mangled or anything. That's better than some people are doing around here." She sat up as if she'd solved a complicated mathematical problem. "What do you think of that?"

Rudy looked around. It was late; there were only a few lights on. He could see the peaked roofs and frazzled trees of his neighborhood below. The Blazers and Broncos and pickups would be parked down there, some in the driveways, some almost forming walls along the streets. Rudy's father usually sat up late watching television, but even he would be in bed by now. The parking lot was dotted with paper cups and hamburger cartons.

"Is that supposed to make me feel better?" Rudy said. "Because it's not."

Moose

Tommy Rincinaldi shot Bruce Barmusch, the inspector at the landfill, on the Tuesday before Labor Day weekend. He was angry because Barmusch had caught him dumping out-of-town rubbish from his garbage truck. Rincinaldi was known to have a temper and was thought to be slightly crazy. The bullet grazed Barmusch's arm and he dove behind the pile of the offending trash and lay across a pillowlike plastic bag that oozed wet paper and blackened vegetables. After a minute he lifted his head. He was panting. Behind him, the slope of the landfill fell away steeply. Seagulls floated in the distance. The sky was white with sun and haze. A small river, heavily polluted and the color of khaki, curved past the end of the long, man-made barrow, and two garbage trucks trundled toward the gate. Thirty or forty yards in front of Barmusch, at the high point of the landfill, the trash compactor, a huge machine that resembled a dragon on rollers, moved back and forth, belching smoke each time it changed direction.

There were two other trucks and several cars at the dumping front. Perhaps ten people had seen the shooting. Barmusch noticed Donald Stowe running toward him. He had jumped down from the scraper—the Caterpillar machine that distributed soil over the garbage in finished cells of the landfill. He was a small, bowlegged man in his early sixties. It was risky to run here; a foot could sink suddenly; it was easy to break an ankle. When Stowe reached the end of the compacted area, he picked his way carefully, sometimes bogging down to his knees in the loose soil and trash. He was breathing hard when he bent over Barmusch, and Barmusch stared at the sunburned top of his head. Stowe had had a heart attack that spring and had returned to work in July.

"I'm sick of this crap!" Rincinaldi yelled. "I am sick of all this crap!"

Barmusch's legs jerked involuntarily, and he put his head in his arms for a moment. "Don't tell him nothing," he told Stowe, looking up. "I want him to think I'm dead."

"Rincinaldi, you're an idiot!" Stowe yelled over the garbage.

"I'm sick of this shit!"

"What's he doing now?" Barmusch asked.

"Sitting on his bumper."

After a minute, they heard Rincinaldi's truck driving away.

The truck was found abandoned later that afternoon at Kentucky Fried Chicken; the manager had called the police to complain, because it had been parked there for two hours and was discouraging customers. Rincinaldi turned himself in the following day. He was charged with assault with a deadly weapon, illegal dumping, carrying an unregistered firearm, and threatening. He was released on twenty thousand dollars' bail.

Barmusch's job was necessary because landfills in surrounding towns had been closed and the trash collected there had to be shipped to sites much farther off, at costs ranging from thirty-five to sixty dollars per ton—rates the garbagemen didn't like to pay. The price at the city landfill was eight dollars per ton. Barmusch dug around the edges of each load after it was dumped, looking for envelopes or boxes with addresses on them. There was a lot of cheating—this was the third time, for example, that he had caught Rincinaldi. Barmusch was known, variously, as Officer Obie (from Arlo Guthrie's "Alice's Restaurant" song), Sanford & Son, or Bruce the Moose, a nickname that dated from high school and was a reference to his size and to the pronunciation of his last name. He earned eight-fifty an hour. In February, he had been laid off from the Pratt & Whitney jet-engine-repair plant in Southington, where the pay was twelve-seventy. He was twenty-three and married, and he and his wife had a mortgage.

Barmusch's current ambition was to get a heavy-equipment operator's license. Stowe was thinking of retiring in December. If that happened, Bobby Stanczyk, who drove the compactor, would move over to the scraper, and Barmusch presumably would have a chance at running the compactor. That job paid thirteen-ten.

Stanczyk had promised to give Barmusch lessons late in the afternoon, when the compactor, known informally as Orange Squash, or "the squasher," crushed the last of the day's garbage.

The compactor was an Ingersoll-Rand LF-450. It weighed forty-five thousand pounds and had cost the city a hundred and sixty-two thousand dollars. Instead of wheels, it had four rollers that were four feet across and covered with spikes. The rollers were silver and rust-colored in spots, and the rest of the machine was a bright orange. The first time Barmusch saw the compactor, he thought it belonged on the cover of a record album by some heavy-metal rock group.

When he drove it for the first time, he was surprised by the instability of the garbage beneath the machine. It had a swampy texture and extended in all directions like a lake—a lake on the top of a hill. From up there the roofs of houses could be seen a half mile away. The trash looked different than it did down at the dumping front. There it appeared as separate mounds that were soon bulldozed into a wall five or six feet high. You saw only the edge of the garbage; you didn't realize how far back it extended.

"How do you know when enough's enough?" he bellowed. It was almost four on the Thursday after Labor Day. The landfill had closed at three-thirty. It was necessary to yell in order to be heard over the engine. Usually the driver wore earmuffs.

"You sort of stop sinking after a while," Stanczyk said, from his perch behind the operator's seat. He was standing up, holding on to a bar across the roof. He was in his mid-twenties and wore a Red Sox baseball cap. "After you go over the same stuff five or six times, you can tell. Sometimes it takes nine or ten. We're still sinking."

Barmusch felt the squasher tip from side to side, like a boat. "Get the blade way up when you don't need it," Stanczyk said. "It's fragile and there's big lumps of junk out there you don't want to hit. Refrigerators and stuff. They get in there even though they aren't supposed to be in there."

Barmusch raised the bulldozerlike blade, but couldn't see how Stanczyk could distinguish what was all right from what wasn't all right. There was a lot of garbage to look at—often it billowed high in front of the cab and they seemed to be driving into the middle of it. Then the compactor would hit the slope and climb steeply, like a tank treading up a riverbank. Barmusch would find himself staring at sky.

"Tommy Rincinaldi came around again today," he told Stanczyk. "He tipped his trash, and while he was doing that he made a pistol with his hand and pointed it at me."

Barmusch had a bandage on his left forearm where Rincinaldi's bullet had hit him.

"He's going to jail," Stanczyk said. "Let's see him be a wise-ass there."

The right front roller hit something and the steering wheel wrenched hard to the left. Barmusch lost his grip, and the whole machine tilted. He jerked his foot from the pedal, stopping everything. The squasher had no foot brake or clutch. When the pedal was pushed in, the machine moved. A hand lever determined the direction: forward or reverse. Barmusch was half out of his seat, his shoulder against the left window of the cab. Stanczyk put one hand on his arm, steadying him. Barmusch nervously switched off the engine.

"It's like that," Stanczyk said, his voice unexpectedly loud without the engine roar. "If you hit something, it turns." He and Barmusch looked around for a moment. Beyond the window, on the left, was a pit some seven or eight feet deep; they were tilted toward it. In front of them soared a mound of trash, a gelatinous mix of colors with browns and whites predominating. It was very hot. Flies buzzed at the windshield.

"Set the controls for the heart of the universe," Stanczyk said. "Let's blast out of here."

When he got home, Barmusch sank reverently into the bathtub. He took a bath every night, followed by a shower. After a day at the landfill, his skin was actually a different color. His wife, Donna, had put up green curtains and there was a skirt around the water tank of the toilet. Barmusch was still working at the jet-engine-repair plant when they bought the house. It was a small, one-story box, about forty years old, on Evans Street.

Donna came home after a while and came in and sat on the counter by the bathroom sink while they talked about a cookout they had planned for Saturday afternoon.

"You going to wear your American Hero jeans?" she asked, smirking.

"Shut up," Barmusch said, splashing her.

"You don't look as dirty as usual today."

"Well, thank you. Thanks very much."

The jeans dated from last week. The morning after Rincinaldi had shot him, Barmusch had had his picture in the paper, and the day after that, at a City Council meeting, the mayor had given him a citation for distinguished municipal service. Then the Council had voted to raise the tipping fee at the landfill to twenty-five dollars per ton to discourage out-of-town refuse and to avoid, as one member put it, "further violence to our valued employees down there who have to cope with this very unique situation." The day after that, Channel 8 did a news spot on the landfill and the TV reporter asked Barmusch to display the bandage on his arm. That night, as a joke, Donna went out and bought him American Hero jeans. She said they were for a man to wear when his day's work was done and he'd put his life on the line defending the city's garbage.

Barmusch hadn't been happy about the publicity. It had been difficult. He didn't like being known as a garbage inspector, and the shooting had frightened him more than he had admitted to anybody. He had nightmares.

"Stowe's looking pretty good," he said, soaping his shoulders. "He might stay on another two years, till he's sixty-five."

"Did you ask him to come Saturday?"

"I asked him. I don't have any idea if he'll come or not."

Donna said, "You should get off this bulldozer kick, Moose, and take more courses at Middlesex. You may never get to drive that thing."

Barmusch had taken introductory chemistry at

Middlesex Community College the previous fall and
had hated it. He had barely graduated from high school.
His grades had never been very good, and his last year
there he'd started hanging around with Rico Landona, a
football teammate who lived in a housing project by the
rail line between New Haven and Hartford. Landona
would get up to a hundred and twenty on Interstate 91
at three in the morning, in cars he said deserved reaching what he called their "true potential." Barmusch
never participated in the stealing of these automobiles,
but he knew he was guilty in a sense by riding with
Rico once he'd stolen them. Landona would see how
fast a car could go, and then he would return it to the
general area from which he'd taken it, claiming it was
satisfied. Barmusch didn't get much sleep that winter
and spring, and he flunked a current-events course and
received his diploma only after he wrote an extra paper
that raised the grade to a D.

Landona was in prison now. He never sent letters,
but sometimes he called Barmusch up. Donna didn't
like these phone calls. The last one was just before
Christmas. "You're at Middlesex Community," Landona said. "I'm at Enfield State. I don't know about
you, but we're studying license plates."

Barmusch sometimes chanted to himself, "Dozer
. . . scraper . . . squasher." At some point before it
got too cold, he wanted to drive each of them. Saleski
handled the bulldozer; he was usually at the bottom
working with the piles of scrap metal that would be
shipped to Japan for recycling and with the brush pile

that eventually would be run through the Highway Department's woodchipper. He also pushed and carved at the landfill slope, using old construction material as a bed for the roads needed to open new fronts on the dumping site.

The landfill entrance was in front of the metal pile, near the truck scale and a mobile home that had a couple of old couches inside. Doris Masci, a heavy woman in her fifties, sat at the desk by the trailer's sliding window and read the scale and took the money from the drivers. The drivers had nicknamed her Tinker Bell. There was a bumper sticker popular in town that read "No FAT CHICKS," and Sol Rincinaldi, Tommy Rincinaldi's brother, had one on the door of his truck. Sometimes he pretended to cover it with one hand as he drove past the window. Doris also had a walkie-talkie. By the time Barmusch had found an out-of-town garbage violation, the offender was often on his way down the hill; Barmusch would radio Doris and when the truck stopped to be reweighed on the way out she would close the gate. The driver had to hand over his landfill permit and reload the trash—a dirty, time-consuming job that usually required the offending company to send over an extra hand or two to help. On his way out, the driver would be given a bill for five hundred dollars. Truck owners often appealed the fine, claiming a few envelopes with out-of-town addresses on them weren't enough to prove they were guilty. Frequently they got off—the city wouldn't press charges. Since the landfill fee had been raised, there had been less cheating. It was hot for September; the sun was relentless—nothing grew except some thin grass on the sections that had been soiled over for a year—and the wind whipped scraps of paper around. Overhead, the seagulls flapped and squawked. Visitors were oppressed by the smell of the landfill, but the employees were used to it.

Sol Rincinaldi's truck arrived at the dumping front. It was lime-green and had a large daisy painted on the side. Below were the words "DAISY-FRESH CARTING." (Cute names were in vogue; also working in the city were Supertrash, Inc., and Little Flower Refuse Removal Co.) The green on Sol's truck was blackened noticeably toward the back. His father owned the firm, and there were eight trucks; they had routes in six towns in central Connecticut. Tommy Rincinaldi still came and went regularly while awaiting trial. He had shown no remorse over the shooting. He and Barmusch would trade angry, obscene gestures, and after each visit Barmusch would search Rincinaldi's trash scrupulously.

Shortly after Sol had tipped his garbage and driven away, Barmusch noticed, at the edge of the pile, a large glass jar that contained a human hand. He kicked at a box behind it and a torn seam widened. An eye stared back at him. He discovered an entire head in there, gray-blue in color, with the hair shaved off and intricate stitching down the cheeks. On one side the stitches curved up under the brow. Barmusch walked a short distance away and bent over. He realized after a minute that he wasn't going to be sick. It was a blue eye. He called Doris on the walkie-talkie and then waved his arms at Stanczyk. It took a minute before Stanczyk saw him and drove the trash compactor off the accumulated garbage and onto the clearing and stopped. The engine was idling gutturally.

"Can you repeat that?" Barmusch yelled over his walkie-talkie.

"He said that garbage is all local," Doris said over the radio. "He said you're crazy. He said you got some kind of vendetta."

"He didn't stop?"

"He said you can send the cops after him, he doesn't care."

When Stanczyk had looked in the box, he said, "That ain't supposed to be here."

Barmusch was trying to breathe deeply and to keep staring at the horizon.

"Like, a year ago?" Stanczyk said. "Before you were working here? I was running the squasher one day and I went over all these plastic bottles. They looked like big white milk jugs. And suddenly there were all these needles sticking up. You could've walked over them and completely skewered your feet. There were thousands of them, like grass. I can't believe what people bring here."

"We should call up the Highway Department," Barmusch said. "Tell Venturi. Somebody should get in trouble for this."

"Venturi won't do nothing," Stanczyk said. He had his earmuffs around his neck.

"We should get him over here to look at it, at least," Barmusch said. "He's never over here and he never gets the cops over here. It'd give me pleasure just to see him look at it."

After a while, Stowe stopped the scraper and came over to find out what was going on. After Stanczyk told him, the two of them leaned against the compactor and lit cigarettes. When Stowe offered the pack to Barmusch, Barmusch backed off, clutching his stomach. "If I had one of those right now, you'd see something else that was ugly," he said. "I'd be imitating a volcano, right here at the dump."

"Moose, you work here a few years and you'll be able to look at anything and not get upset," Stowe said.

"You thinking of retiring, Donald?" Barmusch asked irritably. "So I can drive the compactor and not get used for target practice or finding people's heads or any of this other crap?"

Stowe looked up, surprised. "I haven't thought about it for a couple of weeks," he said. "Don't get mad at me, Moose. It's not my fault."

"You should retire and take trips, Donald," Barmusch said. "Spend more time at Mr. Lazy's."

Mr. Lazy's had exotic dancers. Stowe was known to go there occasionally. He was divorced.

"Shut up, Moose," Stanczyk said. "Where're your manners?"

"I just want to know if he's retiring or not," Barmusch said.

"Trips," Stowe said. "Right. I'm the kind of guy that takes trips. Who takes trips around here? Where've you ever taken a trip?"

"Bridgeport," Barmusch said.

"Cut it out," Stanczyk said, thumping Barmusch on the shoulder. "Tell him you're sorry."

Barmusch exhaled, shaking his head rapidly to clear it, and then took a deep breath. "Sorry, Donald," he said. That evening he called Stowe and apologized again.

The cookout began at two. It was a bad time—it was very hot and the yard had little shade. Barmusch and Stanczyk had set up lawn chairs and two folding card tables next to the picnic table, and the stereo had been moved into the kitchen and the speakers placed against the screen windows facing the backyard. Friends Barmusch and Donna had gone to high school with and a few of Barmusch's buddies from Pratt & Whitney were invited, and Donna had asked people from her office, which was the local branch of Connecticut Light & Power Co. Several couples came with children, who tried for a while to play croquet. The men threw Frisbees and a softball, but ultimately the beer and heat left everyone sitting in the glare as if stunned. Donna had made a lot of potato salad, which was set out in large bowls, and Barmusch cooked hamburgers and hot dogs at the grill, which he'd started by blasting the charcoal with a blowtorch. As the afternoon passed, a sizable group ended up in the living room, which had air-conditioning.

About four-thirty, Barmusch was summoned to the phone. It was noisy in the kitchen, and he stepped onto the cellar stairs and closed the door against the phone cord. It was Sol Rincinaldi.

"We're busy," Barmusch said.

"Sorry," Rincinaldi said. "I figured we needed to talk."

"I knew you guys were into shooting people," Barmusch said, "but I didn't know you cut their heads off afterward."

"We got to stop this," Rincinaldi said. "I'm telling you the truth. I started that route yesterday in Cheshire. It was a mistake, but we're rearranging the routes and some of them are a little messed up right now. It was like four or five houses. I thought if I call up and level with you you'll be understanding and we can stop this feud that got started between you and my brother. It was only a few houses in Cheshire. Then Mrs. Masci tries to close the gate on me. I'm not ready to pay no five-hundred-dollar fine for a few houses."

"You should have been arrested."

"We can't check everything that goes into the truck," Sol said. "That's all I'm saying. I wouldn't've driven away if I knew that was the problem."

"You're a real noble guy, Sol," Barmusch said.

"I think the police are going to call you. They were trying to call people all morning. You guys should fine somebody over this. You should fine somebody besides working people who are trying to make a living."

Shortly after that, Venturi, the Highway Department superintendent, called. "You'll have to come over to the landfill for a few minutes," he said.

"I have guests."

"Well, there's a meeting set up. I can't change it now."

"Do I get paid for this?"

"Bruce," Venturi said. "You guys wanted me to do something, I'm doing something. Now get over here. It'll take about twenty minutes."

The road to the landfill went past heavy-equipment yards, a couple of antique stores, an American Legion post with a weedy baseball field, an abandoned silver-plating factory collapsing in a bed of sumac trees, and several junkyards. The landscape baked steamily in the heat, but the trees, grass, and sumac bushes softened the effect of the glinting metal. Then came the vast tan dust dune of the landfill. With nothing moving anywhere, no bustle out of the junkyards and no trucks climbing to the dumping site, it was revealed as a forlorn and godforsaken place, a place no one wanted to visit or even think about on a Saturday afternoon. The gate was open and Barmusch drove up the rutted, cratered road. The compactor was parked near the top, and three cars nosed into its shadow. One was a police cruiser. After Barmusch parked, Venturi introduced him to a vice-president of the local hospital, a man named Kavanaugh. Kavanaugh wore a knit golf shirt.

"Where did you find it?" the policeman asked Barmusch.

Barmusch explained that the site was covered up, but pointed to the general location. Shadows from the seagulls circling overhead made moving patterns on the soil around their feet.

"You're sure it was Rincinaldi's truck?"

"Didn't he say so?"

"He didn't admit anything. He just said he picked up at the hospital."

"Yeah, it was his truck."

Venturi pointed at a plastic garbage sack held down with rocks by the right rear roller of the compactor. "Do you want to see it?" he asked Kavanaugh.

"Not especially," Kavanaugh said, but he went over and looked.

The policeman said to Barmusch, "Was that the only place you could put it?"

"What do you want me to do, take it home and stick it in the refrigerator?" Barmusch said. "Everybody seems to think we're responsible for this thing, but it's not even supposed to be here. Why don't you keep it at the police station if you're so worried about it?"

"Calm down, Moose," Venturi said.

Kavanaugh returned. "That's ours," he said tiredly. "Plastic surgeons do that sometimes. They practice on cadavers. They had a session Wednesday. Did you dig up any others?"

"No," Barmusch said.

"Good," Kavanaugh said. He explained that the hospital incinerator was down. "The other thing, the hand, that's theirs, too. All that stuff's supposed to go to Hartford. Somebody got lazy. If I can figure out who it is, I'll fire him."

There was a collective shifting of feet. Kavanaugh looked at the plastic bag, then walked over and picked it up. He put it on the floor by the rear seat of his Chrysler LeBaron and drove off.

There were still a few people in the backyard when Barmusch got home. One of them was Stowe—he was sitting at the picnic table talking to Donna. He was a good thirty years older than anyone else who had come.

"This is the guy who called Tommy Rincinaldi an idiot," Barmusch said. "I'm lying facedown in the garbage and Rincinaldi's holding a gun and Donald's standing there calling him an idiot."

Stowe took a gulp from his beer and told Donna he'd had his heart attack on a cold day when he was in the trailer with a cup of coffee. He'd been rushed to the hospital and the emergency-room physician had given him a new drug that dissolved blood clots. Later his cardiologist said it had saved his life. "After that, I'm not afraid of anything," he said.

"That's weird," Donna said. "Since he got shot, Moose is afraid of everything. He's been having nightmares."

"Donna," Barmusch said.

"Rincinaldi's crazy," Stowe said, "but he's only crazy up to a point."

"Point where he shot me," Barmusch said.

"Not for a five-hundred-dollar fine. He was trying to miss. He's just a bad shot. Fine him a thousand, he might've tried to kill you and missed. Instead he was trying to get close. That's when he's dangerous."

Barmusch thought about it and decided Stowe was right. It fit the spooky way Rincinaldi had looked. He had looked off to the side when he fired. There hadn't been any eye contact. The pistol, the hand, had seemed erratic and independent of the rest of him. Then the flame—there really was a small flame—and a tearing sensation in his arm. The arm had been flung backward. Hamburger across his forearm. It looked like a bad rope burn.

"You know what the sick thing about it is, I was almost hoping someone had been murdered," Barmusch told Donna as they were getting into bed that night. "Instead of this hospital stuff with the cadaver head. I was hoping for something exciting."

"What is it with you?" Donna said. "Why do you expect work to be exciting? That's why it's work. That's why they pay you. It's supposed to be boring. Why do you expect everything to be exciting around here? You're the same guy who's been having nightmares because things got exciting."

"I get mixed up," Barmusch said.

Donna turned over. Her back was to him.

"That was the thing with Rico Landona, right?" she said. "Excitement all the time?"

Once again Barmusch had trouble sleeping, and he found himself reverting to the bedtime thoughts he'd had as a child. He imagined ships throbbing through the night, freight trains rumbling invulnerably through blizzards, airplanes droning—huge machines like friendly beasts doing the work of the world, guided by responsible men who stayed up while everyone else slept.

CAMARO CITY

B RUNET, the assistant fleet manager, was putting a replacement barrel on one of the spare concrete-mixing trucks. He was out in the sun and dust of the quarry attaching a crane cable so that the old barrel could be lifted off, and he was talking to Noonan, the youngest driver, who was going to be using the truck for the next few weeks. It was an '81. Two of the '83s were being overhauled, and the new Oshkosh-McNeilus the company had ordered wouldn't arrive for another ten days, assuming the McNeilus people were ready. McNeilus added the mixing equipment.

"You better take care of this," Brunet said. "And remember to spray the damn thing." Drivers were supposed to wash the trucks after each delivery with a mild acid solution to remove the grit and preserve the paint, but they often skipped the chore.

Larry Mohr was running the crane. He had been appointed Brunet's boss in the spring, although he was some ten years younger. (This was a family firm, cur-

currently run by Mohr's uncle, George Loughery.) Brunet was in his mid-thirties, a blond, wide-faced, thick-waisted man a little over six feet tall. There had been a fire at his house Friday night—a fairly serious fire that apparently had started with a malfunction of the furnace—and he was in a bad mood, and after a few minutes Noonan escaped and went over to the crane and began to joke around with Mohr, who had been a friend since high school.

It was October. The sumac bushes had turned scarlet above the rim of the quarry, and fringes of yellow grass frothed over the edge. There was the sense of an extreme landscape here, although this wasn't exactly a mountain and it was made dramatic only by blasting. The quarry was a large bite taken from the side of a ridge, one of the low, crumbling spines that run north-south through Connecticut. In another ten years, the explosives and the front-end loaders would eat their way completely through it.

Brunet wrestled at the undercarriage of the truck with a wrench. Where he stood in the quarry, not far from the entrance but out of sight of the road, was an informal junkyard. A dozen old cement-truck drums, some of them twenty feet long, were jumbled like giant Easter eggs among rusted pieces of superstructure from the conveyor belts, jettisoned diesel engines, and old buckets from the front-end loaders. Noonan and Mohr watched a company pickup drive up. It stopped next to Brunet, and Kobliski, one of the dispatchers, got out and said something. He had his hands in his bluejeans pockets. After a minute, Brunet began to throw pieces of traprock at the nearest abandoned barrel. He threw nine or ten rocks, and the deep gongs they made when he connected (he missed once or twice) could be heard over the idling of the crane. Then he went back to work while Kobliski waited in the cab of the pickup. After ten minutes, the old barrel came free and dangled from the crane, and Brunet got into the cab and drove the truck out from beneath it.

"Goddam it!" he yelled when he got out, because Mohr seemed in no hurry to let the barrel down; it was white and had blue stripes, and said "MOHR CONCRETE & TRAPROCK" in large red letters. It glinted like a huge, battered Christmas-tree ornament. Brunet gestured impatiently, but Mohr had backed off from the controls and was exchanging a joke with Noonan, and after a minute Brunet got into the pickup and drove off.

Someone had stolen his Camaro. His wife had called Kobliski and told him to tell Brunet that he was supposed to meet a policeman in the parking lot by the company office at ten-thirty. When Brunet got there, he found that the cop had come not so much to obtain specific information as to lecture him. The car was a red 1986 Berlinetta, Brunet said. There were three hundred dollars' worth of tools in the trunk. It had twenty-two thousand miles on it and was in good condition. The officer, a Sergeant DeFrances, said, "Don't buy another one." He explained that the town had gotten a reputation among professional car thieves. They called it Spudville and Camaro City. Brunet had heard the term "spud" used by the quarry's younger employees—it meant that a person was shaped like a potato and about as intelligent.

It was true that the number of Camaros in town seemed to suggest a local ordinance. They clotted the parking lots of the videocassette outlets, while kids from the high school talked through the rolled-down windows. (This wasn't a rich community, and Brunet didn't understand how teenagers could afford them.) Basketball-bellied men in their fifties heaved themselves out of the low seats of the cars at midnight and went into the doughnut shops carrying police-band radios and wearing camouflage jackets and multicolored baseball caps. Infants were driven around town in Camaros, straitjacketed into the safety chairs the state now required.

Sergeant DeFrances had so much equipment on his hips that his shoulders looked disproportionately narrow, like a woman's. He leaned against his cruiser and consulted a clipboard. The Camaro had been taken, apparently in daylight, from the parking lot of the Ramada Inn, where Brunet and his wife and two daughters were staying while their house was being repaired. (Brunet explained that he always drove his Nissan pickup truck to work, because the grit that floated around the quarry was bad for the Camaro's paint.) His was the fifty-sixth Camaro stolen since January, in a city with a population of sixty thousand.

"These guys come off I-91, and yours was right next to the highway, for God's sake," DeFrances said. "They must think everyone in town is an idiot." He said the car was probably in Bridgeport or the Bronx by

now, where it would be broken down into parts or re-
painted so that it could be driven South and sold. There
were used-car dealers in Tennessee and Alabama who
didn't ask too many questions.

"I can tell you guys are going to be a big help,"
Brunet said to him. "What the hell business is it of
yours what kind of car I drive? You're supposed to get
it back."

"If we get it back, which I doubt, at least put a kill
switch in it," DeFrances said. "What is it about Camaros around here? I counted six of them just driving
over here."

"We can't afford Corvettes," Brunet said.

When he returned to the quarry, Mohr and Noonan
waved their arms. "You drove off without one of your
balls!" Mohr yelled, pointing at the barrel.

Brunet slammed the door on Kobliski's truck and
went over to the empty chassis of the Oshkosh. After a
minute, Mohr came over and put a hand on his shoulder. Kobliski had apparently told him about the car.
Brunet gritted his teeth; he had the feeling this was going to be sappy.

"Sorry, Bill," Mohr said. "I didn't know all this
stuff was happening to you, out on the street."

Brunet and his wife, Janice, had planned to look for
a new house in the spring—something in one of the
suburban east-side neighborhoods—and for several
months before the fire, as if feeling guilty about leaving
the area in which he had grown up, Brunet had had
occasional daydream images of himself falling off Vale

Street hill: the incline grew nightmarishly steep and he went all the way to the bottom, as Tom Paulwicz's Monte Carlo had done in July when the parking brake failed. The Monte Carlo was evidence once again that it was dangerous to park on Vale Street, although quite a few people did. Others parked on their lawns. No one seemed tempted to own fewer automobiles. Most households had at least three.

The houses here were from forty to eighty years old, a few of them two-family and three-family. They were tall and close together. The slope of the river valley in which the city lay was steep in this one place, and from the upper part of Vale Street, where Brunet's now charred house stood, there was a tree-obscured view of the vast, tarred roof of a failed shopping mall, four church steeples, two concrete high rises containing senior citizens' apartments, and an old foundry that was being decked by a wrecking ball. The more immediate vista was of small pickup trucks, with all-terrain vehicles or motorcycles strapped to their beds, chain-link fences, and brightly colored fibreglass wedges that turned out to be power boats grounded on the tilted lawns. Men had once walked from here to work at the old silver factories, and postmen still referred to Vale Street as the immigrant Alps, or the Irish Alps, or the Polish Alps.

On the night of the fire, the road was lined with old furniture and kitchen appliances, which had been set out in defiance of an announcement by the city that there wouldn't be a bulky-waste pickup this year. The project was too costly, the mayor had said, but people who had large items to throw away could take them to a municipal transfer station on the west side of town. An informal revolt had spread. As they lugged things up from their basements, people on Vale Street told each other that when the city councillors got tired of the mess they would send crews around to pick it up.

Brunet's berm of junk was the first topic raised by the fire captain Friday night, after Brunet had arrived to find his house filled with water. "If you want to do something stupid," the captain said, "that's a good choice. Someone could die in the time it takes us to run hoses through that."

Frank Morjassian, who lived in the next house up, had smelled smoke around eight-fifteen. When he approached through the side yard, he heard alarms beeping and could see flames through a basement window. He broke in the front door using an aluminum softball bat and lumbered from room to room through the smoke to see if anyone was inside. He smashed most of the upstairs windows, and finally came out coughing and went to his house to call the Fire Department.

While this was going on, Janice was playing in a concert with the local symphony (she was in the back row of the first violins, three seats over from the front of the stage), and Brunet was in the audience at the high-school auditorium, along with their twelve-year-old daughter, Polly, and Alexandra Alfaz, who was ten and lived across the street and took violin lessons from Janice. Brunet endured these events three times a year. Dick Alfaz, Alexandra's father, came and found him at intermission and told him about the fire. He asked anxiously about Brunet's other daughter, Patty, who was fifteen, and Brunet said that as far as he knew she was at the movies, twenty miles away in East Hartford.

When Brunet got there, Vale Street was blocked at the top by a police cruiser, and he had to walk the last three blocks. When he reached the house, it was being bludgeoned by two thick streams of water, which entered where the first story had been axed open on the uphill side. The house looked sodden enough to burst, like a cardboard box put under a faucet. It was hard to believe that anything ever could have been burning in there, although Brunet could see that the windows were gone and the lower frames were charred around the edges.

The crowd that had gathered included a number of Hispanics—the city's Puerto Rican community was encroaching on the bottom of the hill, something that upset many of Brunet's neighbors—and he saw Doug Androskos angrily ordering a group of them out of his front yard. Elsewhere, children yelled and ran about, skirting and leaping over the curbside junk, and neighborhood dogs roamed freely. Frank Morjassian was standing by the Alfazes' driveway, still holding the softball bat. "I did what I could," he told Brunet.

Janice had driven Polly home, and she and Brunet put the girl to bed in Alexandra Alfaz's room. Then they sat in the Alfazes' kitchen. "I don't care," Janice told Brunet. "I hated the place anyway." Patty didn't come home until midnight, and by then they had grown very worried, although the firemen assured them there had been no one in the house.

The family spent the night with Janice's sister and her husband, who lived four blocks away, and at noon Saturday Brunet went back to the house to meet his insurance agent and the city fire marshal.

In the morning, Janice went over the family's finances with Brunet. She was an accountant at the hospital. It was a pattern around here for young women to attend one of the state universities, and then come home, find jobs, and marry men they had known since high school—men who worked in construction and might have worked in the factories if the factories hadn't closed. Janice told Brunet that as long as the insurance settlement was reasonable they could still buy a new house in the spring. She badly wanted to move. "Don't get cold feet now," she said. "Let's just fix it and go."

But Brunet felt viscerally wounded when he saw the house, and he began to have second thoughts. It was his house, and in the daylight it looked terrible, and he felt the full extent of his attachment to it. The smell coming from the windows reminded him of the cement fireplaces in the city parks, which were routinely filled with wet soot, garbage, and broken glass.

Murray Southerland, the insurance agent, sat in the sun on the rear steps and explained that the fire marshal and his assistant were in the basement, ankle-deep in water. They had driven up in a red station wagon with the city insignia on the door and had taken a stepladder down with them. They were inspecting the furnace with flashlights.

Without standing, Southerland handed Brunet five

hundred dollars in cash. "There's a fifteen-hundred-dollar check in that envelope, too," he said, "but I figured you can't cash it on a Saturday afternoon. You're going to need clothes right away."

The sunlight was sharp, and leaves flashed on the trees and drifted down in handfuls. Things were happening. Morjassian, a hefty man who drove a truck for a meat-packing firm, was putting sealant on his driveway, while his little girl sat on the curb wearing an orange T-shirt that read "My Daddy Drives a Harley-Davidson"—and Brunet realized that applying sealant, a fall ritual in the neighborhood, was something he wasn't going to be doing this year. Janice was across the street at the Alfazes', whose lawn bore a new "FOR SALE" sign. Alfaz and his brother had been trying to buy a motel on the Franey Turnpike, and apparently they had succeeded. Dick Alfaz had said property values along the turnpike were going up, and between the two families it wouldn't be necessary to hire outside employees, or for him or his brother to quit their jobs. They were Syrian immigrants. Brunet often drove out on the turnpike early in the morning to get supplies from Bohlan's Truck Parts, and he had noticed small clumps of Indian or Pakistani children outside the motels, standing at the edge of the divided highway with lunchboxes, awaiting the school bus. The Alfazes weren't the only ones to have this idea.

When Fire Marshal Waddell came out, he said the furnace exhaust apparently had fallen away from its connection to the chimney. The pipe was old and had corroded where the two were joined. Brunet admitted he had never replaced it—it had probably been there fifty years. He said the furnace had been turned on Wednesday after being off all summer. Waddell told him that once the connection was broken, hot smoke had accumulated and probably had set boxes or papers burning. He said it was all right for Brunet to take a look around, as long as he watched his step.

The kitchen, a newer room that branched off the rear of the house, felt firm underfoot, but the linoleum had blackened and puffed up like an omelette. They went through the kitchen door, glanced into the living room, where a hole had been chopped in the floor, and then went gingerly up the back stairs, which were covered with water and soot and fallen plaster. On the second floor the walls were black from the smoke, but the door to the girls' room, at the rear of the house, was closed, and when Brunet kicked it open he found an oasis of color: pale-blue walls, tacked-up photos from *Seventeen* and *Sassy,* yellow curtains.

"Things turn out better if you don't smash the windows and if you keep the doors shut," the assistant marshal said.

"This guy with the bat," Waddell said. "You had some bad luck there. I don't know where the idea comes from, but people like to smash things during fires. This fire's just dying to breathe, and some guy comes along and knocks out the glass. I guess it's because they see firemen doing it, but the thing is, the firemen are putting out the fire. They're making holes for the hoses and stuff."

Brunet stared—the curtains were a little discolored. That was it.

Outside, Waddell said he'd finish his written report

in a week or so. He and his assistant drove off, and Southerland leaned against the hood of his Volvo and told Brunet that he was fully covered and that he and Janice should make a list of their possessions and be as specific as possible about the value. The house was insured for eighty thousand—probably less than it would cost to replace it but more than enough to cover the damage.

"Listen to this one," Brunet said when Janice came over. He explained about the windows, and when he was done Southerland told them, "Don't worry about it. You could get just as mad about the water, and Waddell didn't even mention that. The Fire Department always uses five times as much as it has to."

When Southerland was gone, Brunet and Janice got into the Camaro, but Brunet didn't start the engine. He sat there for a moment. When he looked at his hands on the wheel, he noticed that his arms were shaking. "You're a moron!" he bellowed out the window at Morjassian—a fat, bearded figure standing in his driveway and holding a squeegee covered with black muck. Morjassian and his little girl looked up curiously. "I couldn't even explain it," Brunet said to Janice. "He's probably convinced he did me a favor."

"Let's go find a motel," Janice said. "Let's get out of this slum."

Tuesday, when all sixteen drivers were out and the only truck left in the yard was a spare 1975 rear-loader that Brunet considered little more than a curiosity, Noonan called in on his radio and said he was out of gas in Rocky Hill, a half mile short of his delivery point. It was the kind of offense a driver could be fired for, although Noonan claimed that the gas gauge on the truck was broken. Brunet and Larry Mohr put a barrel of fuel into the back of a pickup, strapped it upright, and tossed in a hand pump. It took twenty-five minutes to reach Rocky Hill and another ten to find the truck, which was on a wooded stretch of road between two suburban neighborhoods that hadn't existed when Brunet worked in the area five years ago. He and Noonan pumped the gas in, but the truck wouldn't start—trying to make his destination, Noonan apparently had ignored the initial sputtering and had run it bone dry. The battery was close to dead and Mohr was on the verge of calling for a heavy-duty tow truck—necessary for a vehicle holding almost ten cubic yards of concrete and weighing, with that payload, about seventy-two thousand pounds—when the engine finally caught. By then a second truck had been dispatched to make the delivery, and a good portion of the load carried in Noonan's had dried and set in the barrel. They surreptitiously pumped out the rest and watched it flow down the portable troughs into a thicket of trees. They got the truck back to the yard by five-fifteen, and Brunet brought out the jackhammer. "You know how to use this?" he asked Noonan.

"No."

"Where do they get you guys?" Brunet bellowed.

He told Noonan to go home, and then he unbolted the trapdoor on the side of the drum. The interior had metal fins some ten inches high that spiraled around the inside. Spun in one direction, they forced the wet concrete toward the bottom and rolled it, keeping it well mixed. Turned the other way, they corkscrewed it up and out of the truck through the opening over the cab. The fins were several feet apart and the dried concrete was caked between them; here and there it was as deep as six inches. Brunet gritted his teeth. Everyone who worked at the quarry hated this chore. He began at the bottom, where it was possible to stand upright. He wore goggles, earmuffs, and a breathing mask. By the time he had been in there five minutes, his temples clanged from the noise, and he was sweating heavily and his arms throbbed from wrestling with the jackhammer. At that point, the barrel began to turn. He released the jackhammer and tipped it into the channel between the fins next to him, then leaned forward against the ascending slope as he slid toward the bottom. Clumps of concrete fell over his head and shoulders, and he howled into the respirator, then clawed it off, inadvertently taking his goggles with it. Dust filled his eyes, and he covered his head with his hands. The turning stopped. He noticed dimly that the opening was directly over his head.

He yelled, but there was no response. If the truck had been running a minute ago, it wasn't now. After a few minutes, he climbed over the fins and squeezed out through the narrow port over the cab. He thought he glimpsed a car disappearing behind the trees that lined the road between the office and the quarry entrance, but there was a lot of shadow and his vision was blurred. No one else was in the yard. He had a coughing fit and went into the bathroom in the mechanic's shed and splashed his face and eyes with water. Then he drank in long gulps.

When he came out, George Loughery was there, looking for him. Loughery, Larry Mohr's uncle, was president of the company. He wore a blazer, a white shirt, and gray slacks. He briefly studied the drum of the Oshkosh, which had spun far enough to have pulled the jackhammer hose out of the air compressor. Then he saw Brunet. "I'm the one that takes the phone messages around here after six o'clock," he said. "A Sergeant De-Frances just called. They found your Camaro."

Brunet pounded at the concrete dust on his clothes. It came off in large white puffs. Loughery had written the information on a sheet of paper. The car was in New Rochelle, New York, near a loading dock, he told Brunet. It was missing the engine, the doors, the transmission, the hood, the fenders, the wheels, and the tape deck. Brunet could tell the insurance company it was a total loss.

"I don't think your nephew's up to being fleet manager," Brunet told him, changing the subject.

"I know, I know," Loughery said tiredly. "We can't have him hiring drivers who run out of gas."

"Why don't you make me boss for a while? I'll break him in good."

"I expect you would," Loughery said. He looked back steadily. "This job arrangement is stupid, but there's nothing I can do about it right now. I've got lots of relatives in this company telling me what to do. If you need some money, what with the house and the car, we can work something out."

"The insurance is O.K.," Brunet growled. "Janice

is getting rich anyway. You lay me off in December like you usually do and we'll still be O.K."

"You're mad about this, aren't you?" Loughery said.

"Listen to this one," Brunet told him, pounding more dust from his clothes. He said he thought someone had spun him deliberately in the barrel of the truck. "The only guy I can think of is Noonan," he said, "which would be pretty bad, because I was doing him a favor."

"If he did it, he's fired, but he'll never admit it," Loughery said. "If he runs out of gas again, he's fired anyway."

"It's hard to believe anybody'd do it," Brunet said. "I thought I felt the engine, but I was wearing earmuffs and I was shaking pretty good from the hammer. It didn't go very far. Is there any way it could just happen?"

They talked about it and checked the chain drive on the barrel. There seemed no way it could just happen.

"Him and me are going to have a talk," Brunet said. "And you tell Larry when he gets in that he can chisel the rest of that stuff out. I did my share. That's a brand-new barrel those guys messed up."

"What's all this Spudville stuff about?" Loughery asked. "The cop must've mentioned that five times."

"I really don't like that guy," Brunet said.

Brunet and Janice and the girls ate at Burger King. He had taken a shower and had told Janice about the truck barrel. He thought he felt all right. "I've had nightmares about that happening," he said. "It shakes me up just getting into one of those things."

But it was cheerful in the restaurant. He liked the way the family walked out of the motel each night and over into the fast-food thicket on Sharpe Avenue and picked a place to eat, and he also liked it that the girls seemed happy at the Ramada Inn, where they had their own room and television, and that they enjoyed making nightly trips to the mall for new clothes, courtesy of the insurance company. (Although their room was intact, most of their clothes had gone up with a pair of bureaus in the hall.) He seemed to be the only one who missed the house.

"I still can't believe what Morjassian did," he told Janice. They had finished their hamburgers and the girls were out in the restaurant game room. "Why would someone run around somebody else's house with a baseball bat?"

The table was cluttered with cardboard hamburger cartons and paper cups with plastic tops, and Janice was drawing on the last of a milk shake. "Because he wanted to," she said, waving it at him. "If you're Morjassian, you don't get that many chances to be a good citizen. He's not going to go over there with buckets of water, and he's not going to do charity work or join the Rotary Club or anything. But if he sees a chance to help society out by smashing somebody else's windows, he'll do it."

"You should see it over there," Brunet said. "You never even went inside. The TV's exploded. The picture tube blew up. The phone's melted down the wall. He was a big help, all right."

"Well, I don't know if I should bring this up," Janice said, "but if you buy another Camaro you better not complain about Morjassian."

Brunet stared at her. "I was just starting to relax," he said.

"I'm just pointing it out. Before any decisions get made. Morjassian does stupid things to other people, but if you buy another Camaro you're doing something stupid to yourself. It'll just get stolen."

"I'll buy any car I want to," Brunet said.

"That's what bothers me about that neighborhood," Janice said. "That's why I can't wait to get out of there. That's the sort of thing people say over there. They do stupid things and then they say stupid things to explain why they're doing them."

"Nobody else is going to call me stupid right now," Brunet said. He could feel himself getting hot. "It's bad enough with the cop. This is none of your business."

"I just don't like self-defeating behavior. It reminds me of the way people have junk all over their lawns. The city's never going to pick it up—they're just turning their yards into pigsties for nothing. They're the ones who have to look at it every day. Or there's some accident down the street with a gun and everybody says it's not the gun's fault, or Paulwicz's kid crashes on his Honda ATV and he's in the hospital for three weeks, and now he's out and he's driving the ATV again. The whole neighborhood's that way. The only people who aren't total idiots are Dick and Sophie."

"What'd you marry me for if you think I'm so stupid?" Brunet said. "That's self-defeating behavior, too, right?"

"Don't go," Janice said, because he was standing up.

"You can't be as smart as you think you are, because if you end up with a guy like me you should know Camaros are part of the deal," Brunet said.

"Don't go stomping out of here," Janice said. "It's just a suggestion. It's just something I've been wanting to talk about. If you're that mad, let's drop it. Forget I brought it up."

"I'm not stomping out of here," Brunet said. "I'm taking a walk."

He drank a cup of coffee at a doughnut shop up the street, and found himself staring at two Camaros whose broad hoods nosed over the sidewalk toward the shop. The parking lot was brightly lit. He liked the way Camaros managed to be streamlined and massive at the same time. After he finished his coffee he went outside and stood in front of one of them—the one that wasn't yellow. Brunet didn't think Camaros should be yellow. This one was gold and it had been around for a while. The paint was pitted and the car had several dents, and one of the front fenders was painted with gray primer. The car looked like a veteran airplane, not very glossy but sturdy and likable. The basic shape came through, and it got to him. He could imagine sitting in the low seat, with the engine vibrating against his right leg, which he always leaned against the hump that covered the transmission and drive shaft. There would be the smell of old cigarettes. There would be sunglasses and a lighter in the cubbyhole under the radio, and some empty French-fry packets. As he walked around the side, he was stopped by the sight of his distorted reflection in the corner of the windshield. He said, "Christ," and started back toward the motel. He didn't want anybody to see him like that—a heavy guy staring for five minutes at somebody's old Camaro. He wasn't sure if he and Janice had had a serious argument, but it seemed time for them to move on to the next thing.

BILT·RITE

ILT-RITE CONSTRUCTION, INC., laid off three of its
four employees on the second Friday in August.
They were Steve Heagan, thirty-seven; Paul Mylicki,
twenty-eight, a casual member of the Diablo Bandits
motorcycle gang; and Ronnie Ramsey, twenty-four and
probably the most responsible of the group. Certainly
he was the most vulnerable financially. He was married
and had two kids and a house, and Ralph Correggio,
Bilt-Rite's owner, agonized over how Ramsey and his
wife were going to cover their mortgage.

Heagan, who had worked as a carpenter for twenty
years and had almost gotten into a fistfight recently with
a city building inspector, was in a different position; he
was divorced, childless, and lived in a trailer park on the
Franey Turnpike. He owned his mobile home outright.
Mylicki bounced around. He stayed with his parents,
with various friends, or in apartments and houses the
motorcycle gang sometimes rented.

Rich Lacroix, the company's fourth employee,
wasn't laid off, because he was on workmen's comp. He

had broken his leg in March, when a flat of two-by-fours he was unloading exploded. Lacroix had cut the metal strap that held the boards together, and they had rearranged themselves into a pile of sticks. There was no obvious explanation. The weather was hot for March, and perhaps the wood had expanded after being bound on a cold day in Maine. Or perhaps the boards had gotten wet and had swelled. In any case, Lacroix was almost buried. He suffered bruises and cuts all over his body. He was lucky he wasn't knocked off Bilt-Rite's high-rise truck; when the accident happened, the bed of the truck was at roof level in the Cote Hill subdivision. Lacroix's broken shin mended in time, but he was left with a persistent infection in his leg, and he was on and off work. When he did show up, it was unofficially, and Ralph made up the difference between the compensation payments and Lacroix's regular pay.

Four or five independent carpenters and laborers—men so often subcontracted by Bilt-Rite that they played on the company softball team—were told there would be no more work for them, and Mindy Correggio, Ralph's sister, who helped with paperwork two afternoons a week, also was put out of a job. Mindy took classes at Southern Connecticut State University and found work occasionally as a model. She and Lacroix had a sputtering flirtation going on the days when Lacroix managed to come to work, and Ralph wondered what would happen to these two now that they wouldn't have an automatic excuse to see each other.

One at a time, he summoned Heagan, Ramsey, and Mylicki to his office and told them he was closing the company. It seemed the best way to break the news, but of course the minute Heagan was out the door he told the other two. Ralph was surprised to hear them all mention the softball team. He said that anyone who wasn't too depressed could come to his house that evening for pizza, but it turned out that there was a game at seven-thirty. The Bilt-Rite Construction Commandos played in the C Division of the city league.

"Go ahead," he told Mylicki, the third to ask. Mylicki wanted to know about the rest of the schedule, and Ralph said the league fee was paid, and as far as he was concerned the team could finish the season. Ramsey ran the softball; Ralph was nothing but an occasional sub. "I'll put off the pizza until nine," he said.

Ten or fifteen minutes later, his former employees and several people from QualiTex—which shared the old two-story factory Bilt-Rite rented downtown— were throwing a football around in the parking lot. QualiTex salesmen fleshed out the softball team. They had heard about the layoffs and had come out to commiserate. Men in T-shirts and men in oxford shirts and ties dashed around and insulted each other and drank from a case of beer Ralph had put on the hood of Ramsey's car. The parking lot and equipment yard were surrounded by a fence topped with razor wire, and beyond that were the railroad tracks that ran from New Haven to Springfield. It was sunny and hot, although it had rained heavily that morning. There were puddles on the asphalt, and beyond the fence the sumac trees, which created a jungle every year by the railroad tracks, seemed to be steaming.

"Grobak told Mylicki he should buy an industrial sewing machine," Lacroix said. "Did you hear that?"

Halfway across the lot, Mylicki was yelling at Dave Grobak, the QualiTex materials manager, "I ought to nail your ass! My dignity's insulted!" He was waving a compressed-air nail gun he had taken from the back of his pickup.

"You can wear a little skirt if you want," Grobak told him, grinning.

"QualiTex needs somebody to sew insulating covers for turbines," Lacroix said to Ralph. "Some retired guy was doing it in his basement, but he's in the hospital with a stroke. Mylicki thinks he'll lose his balls if he does any sewing."

Ralph had his back against Ramsey's car, and he could feel the hot metal and glass through his shirt. His face was turned up, and his eyes were closed, and he smiled as Lacroix went on to recount his latest argument with Mindy. "God," he said. "I don't know why, but it's always great hearing about you two."

The six-o'clock softball game, Division B, went off as planned, although the diamond at Sipisky Park was muddy. But the Post Office Rowdies, Division C, didn't show up for their seven-thirty game with the Commandos. "Fuck, fuck, fuck," Mylicki chanted, slamming his bat rhythmically into a puddle by the on-deck circle as he and the others waited. He discovered that he could splash muddy water onto Heagan, who was at the plate rapping out ground balls to the infielders.

Lacroix was hanging around, still unable to play,

and Grobak, at third base, was needling him. "You the company pet or something?" he said. "How come you're the only one who's still got a job?"

Players skidded around, chasing each other and throwing mud in handfuls, and then Grobak was up-ended in a puddle by Mylicki and Heagan, who were yelling, "Dunk the yuppies!" At that point a few of the other QualiTex people retreated to their cars.

When Ralph's former employees surrounded him, he grabbed a bat. "No way," he said. "I only came to help you guys out." He had worried—unnecessarily, it seemed—that some of the softball regulars might not show up, because of the layoffs.

Grobak, laughing and slick with mud, said something to Ramsey and Heagan, and then a bunch of the players ganged up on Mylicki and stripped off his shirt—not a regular orange Commandos team jersey but a T-shirt he'd picked up back when the President was making an issue of flag burning. It had an American flag on the chest, along with the words "Burn this one, asshole!" and it had been popular with motorcycle gangs. While the others held Mylicki down, Grobak tried to burn the shirt with a cigarette lighter, but he couldn't get it to catch.

Ralph Correggio wasn't out of business, exactly. Although it now had no employees and no office, Bilt-Rite was still incorporated and was more or less meeting its debts. Ralph had made two hundred and fifty thousand dollars over the previous three years, and had built and paid for his house, although there was no garage and the upstairs wasn't finished. By mortgaging the house, he was able to meet payments on the fifteen undeveloped acres he owned at Cote Hill. His option to buy fifteen more acres there was abandoned. His wife, Paula, whose job as director of the senior citizens' center paid thirty-five thousand dollars a year (Ralph thought this was unbelievable), was able to cover the mortgage while he worked at whatever small jobs he could scrape up—roof repairs, storm-window replacements, garage-to-bedroom conversions, short-notice labor with his father, Rollo, a plumber—in order to meet the loans on his equipment. The construction forklift (bought used for fifteen thousand dollars), the lift-bed truck (bought used for twenty-five thousand dollars), the various nail guns and air compressors were now in his backyard and basement. His lease downtown expired at the end of the month. That was lucky; the rent would have broken him. There was no way he could sell his equipment; the market was flooded with equipment. Draper Quality Homes and Sagazzi & Sons had gone out of business before Bilt-Rite, and more thoroughly. Ralph, meanwhile, looked with envy at DeConcitti, one of the oldest builders in town and still hanging on, thanks to a contract for public housing for the elderly. Bilt-Rite had tried for that project, too. On an offer of seven hundred and eighty thousand, it had been underbid by a hundred and twenty dollars. That had been the end, Ralph felt, although later, when he had more information, he decided the end really had come a week earlier, when Larry Magnin, the city building inspector, had visited the last of the houses Bilt-Rite had under way at Cote Hill.

That particular morning, Ralph, who didn't like mud, had been standing in the residual glop in the ditch by the foundation where the water would be connected. From down there, little could be seen but dirt, the concrete wall, and the midsummer sky, which was the color of jet exhaust. Presently he heard Magnin complaining, "These are nine inches apart."

Magnin, perched on a ladder, was talking about the staples in the plywood facing on the second floor. The standard building-code interval for nailing off plywood was six to eight inches. Ralph could hear him arguing downward at Heagan, who had done the work. Heagan should have known better; he was the man in charge when Ralph wasn't around.

"I can tell you to nail every two inches if I want to," Magnin said.

"That's about the size of your—"

Magnin came down the ladder with blood in his eye, and Ralph intervened just in time. He walked Magnin over to the Building Department's orange pickup truck.

"I don't talk to morons without an appointment!" Heagan yelled after them. "Call my secretary!"

"This whole thing is simple," Magnin said. "You guys are trying to drive me crazy, right? He wants to see if I'm going to make you put the scaffolds back up and put nails in between the nails, all because of one inch. They're nine inches apart. All of them. Don't tell me that's an accident."

"One inch isn't going to make the house fall down," Ralph said.

Now Mylicki was getting involved. "Have your

attorney talk to my attorney!" he yelled from a second-floor-window space. "Have your massage parlor talk to my massage parlor!"

"If I have to stand here and listen to this I'm going to slug somebody in the mouth," Magnin said.

Ralph and Magnin drove off for a cup of coffee. There were stray boards and scraps of insulation along Cote Hill Road. The insulation looked like pink moss. Weeds had crept into the grass surrounding the two completed houses. The grass itself was just starting to come in. On the far side of the field, maple trees made a lumpish line in the haze. Cote Hill had been the city's last dairy farm.

"If you guys are going to act like this, I can make it tough for you to do business in this city," Magnin said.

"Don't worry about it," Ralph told him. "We'll be out of business in a few weeks."

"I like to get along with people."

"You like to push people around. You made us put bridging all over the Pheasant Creek condos, and there wasn't anything about that in the rules. Now suddenly you're a maniac for rules."

Pollard Street, which skirted Cote Hill, ended by Bess Eaton Donuts, on the corner of Sharpe Avenue. Magnin was listening to Kenny Rogers on his dashboard tape player, and as they turned into the lot he said, "Shut up a minute, this is my favorite part," and reached for the volume knob. Rogers was singing "You Gotta Know When to Hold 'Em," and when Magnin had the truck parked he leaned his head back and closed his eyes. "You ought to pay attention," he said. "There's a lot of wisdom in this song."

Ralph got out of the truck and went into the doughnut shop. He returned a few minutes later and handed Magnin a cup of coffee through the open window. He didn't get back in. Past the parking lot there was a drainage ditch and a fence with a surf of litter at its base, and, beyond that, cars shot like disconsolate rockets along the northbound lanes of I-91. The air was sticky and smelled as if it had passed over a giant French-fry vat (there was a McDonald's across the street), and it seemed to Ralph that all over the city people were irritable with one another and were fed up with what they were doing.

"Just tell me what to do about the nails, O.K.?" he said to Magnin. "I don't care what it is, just make up your mind. When I have to deal with crap like this it makes me so mad I don't care about the serious stuff."

"I don't care if you go out of business," Magnin said. "What do you think of that? I'm just doing my job. I just want to get through the year and take my kids to Disney World at Christmas."

"If you're wondering why Heagan did it, it was probably to get on your nerves," Ralph said. "You're right. That's one of the things I like about him. He knew you'd notice something stupid like that and get mad. But it didn't work too good, because you still managed to get a coffee break out of it. I'm sick of arguing with you guys."

"If you waste my time with this petty shit, I'm going to waste yours, too."

"Waste your time?" Ralph asked. "Heck, we wouldn't dream of it. We're putting the other nails in. Quality is our watchword. It'll take somebody four or five hours and it won't make the house any sturdier, but we're going to do it. In fact, we're going to put six nails in all those places. Then you can come around and tell us to pull five of 'em out."

When Magnin had dropped him back at Cote Hill, Ralph told Heagan to restaple the plywood on his own time—that evening and the next day, if necessary. "You're lucky you're still alive," he said. "He trapped me in his truck and made me listen to Kenny Rogers. That's the worst torture I've ever been through in my life."

Later on, Ralph's wife, Paula, and his father, Rollo, claimed Magnin had taken Ralph to the doughnut shop because he was looking for a bribe. "What did you want him to do," Rollo said, "paint you a sign?"

Ralph said, "Why would he look for a bribe from someone who's three hundred thousand dollars in debt? How much does he think he'd get?"

"Nobody said this guy was smart," Paula said.

"It's a bad sign in a business," Grobak said. "You guys didn't like the people who were moving into the houses. You didn't like your own customers."

"So what?" Ramsey said. "We don't like you, either."

"We don't suffer fools gladly," Mylicki told him, having picked up the phrase somewhere, probably from Lacroix, who came out with lines like that. Mylicki had biker's hair—it reached his shoulders—and a ratty beard. Tattoos extended down each arm past the ends of the short sleeves of his softball jersey.

"You must not like yourself very much," Lacroix told him.

They were crowded around a table at Keegan's Tavern, and there was hardly room for all the beer bottles and elbows. If there was any meaning to the occasion it was that they were trying to remain friends with Grobak, who had been unhappy about being thrown in the mud, as it turned out. He said that when he thought about it later it didn't seem like the usual fooling around—there was something hostile about it. Worse, the pizza party at Ralph's house afterward had ended wildly when Grobak made an obscene remark about J.F.K., and Heagan, to everyone's surprise, attacked him. No one had seen Heagan since, although Grobak said Heagan had called him at work Monday, at QualiTex, to apologize. Lacroix, one of several people trying to break up the fight, had been kicked on his infected shin and had spent four days on crutches. That night Ralph told Paula it had been the worst day of his life. "I throw three people out of work, I have the softball team over to cheer everybody up, and World War Three breaks out."

Ralph thought Keegan's overdid it with the air-conditioning. Shivering, he wondered if he would carry in his stomach for the rest of his life the cold, greasy feeling of finishing out the summer as a part-time player on the company softball team that had outlasted his company. On the far side of the room he could see the green shirts of the Sagazzi & Sons players. Sagazzi was in the A Division and the team actually wore matching baseball pants; Jerry Sagazzi was the shortstop. Ralph would have preferred retirement as a Bilt-Rite softball sub, but Heagan hadn't shown up since the fight, and that meant Ralph was needed in right field.

Keegan's Tavern and Lamertino's Restaurant, which were connected by a hall holding rest rooms and a telephone and a cigarette-vending machine, were on the Sharpe Avenue strip, down the street from Bess Eaton Donuts. As usual, Keegan's was full of construction workers. Many of them were unemployed, but they still wore the uniform. In this part of Connecticut most didn't have biker's hair but a style that wasn't quite as long. When they were out with their girlfriends, it was neatly combed and blow-dried so that it swept sideways above the ears. The men tended toward stone-washed jeans and thermal-underwear tops, some with the sleeves ripped out, and had a way of walking that seemed tired in the legs and hips.

Across the table, Mylicki and Grobak started to laugh, and Mylicki got his hands around Grobak's neck and forced him halfway under the table. He was still after Grobak about his sewing-machine proposal.

"I got a profession," Mylicki said. "When I was a baby, my mother took me on her knee and said, 'Son, I want you to build condos.' " Shaking Grobak, he chanted, "Build 'em cheap, build 'em shitty, build 'em just like DeConcitti."

"We weren't that bad," Ralph objected. All his former employees except Lacroix had worked for DeConcitti at one time or another. The company had a bad reputation, and people were always coming and going.

"If you want somebody to sew, why don't you ask me?" Ramsey said to Grobak, surprising everyone. "I'll do it. I'm fucking desperate."

Ramsey, in black pants and a black vest, was slouched in his chair, his skinny arms and his chest and stomach exposed. His stomach was soft-looking, like a woman's. He had a bizarre habit of wearing leather vests, or muscle shirts, or T-shirts cut off above the navel, such as football players wear. He must have weighed a hundred and forty pounds. He had long black hair. "You're really knocking the girls out," Lacroix often told him.

They got up to go, and Ralph swung by the men's room. On the way out he got into an argument with Tony Pintone, an outraged-neighbor type who had opposed the Pheasant Creek condos Bilt-Rite had finished in the spring. Half the units were unsold and had been repossessed by the bank.

"You guys should be in jail," Pintone said. He was buying cigarettes.

"You don't like 'em, why don't you pay me to tear 'em down?" Ralph said.

Pintone had started a Bee Avenue neighbors' group to fight the condo project. The group had delayed the job for a year by objecting to condos in an R-1 zone, but finally the Planning and Zoning Commission had given Bilt-Rite a variance; the P.Z.C. was always siding with builders back then. Pintone was still upset about the ruling, and also about the way he had been treated. Once, at a public meeting, Ralph had called him "Pintone, or Flintstone, or whatever your name is."

"I didn't see your Turkish-whorehouse Cadillac in the lot," Ralph said now. "Did you sell it?"

"You guys should be shot," Pintone told him, but then Ramsey and Mylicki came along, and it was over.

"I hate that guy!" Ralph yelled when they were outside. "Where's his car? I'm going to piss on the door."

"He wouldn't notice. It's a piss-colored car," Lacroix said. "Let's throw some rocks."

Instead, they climbed into their pickups and drove off, one after the other. Ralph wondered when they'd see each other again. An acid haze drifted along the tops of buildings and telephone poles as he turned onto Sharpe Avenue. The city seemed trapped in gray, overcooked air, even at night. After a few blocks, Ralph recognized in his mood the same dread he'd felt as a child late in the summer, when school loomed just ahead. Back then, too, the last August weather had seemed to announce that the fun had gone on for too long and everyone was going to suffer.

In September, Mylicki rode his motorcycle to Florida to look for work. He had a brother there. No one had heard from Heagan. Ralph replaced a garage roof, helped his father with a few plumbing tasks, then spent three weeks reconditioning boilers at a factory in Naugatuck—it was a QualiTex customer, and Grobak had got him the job. Ralph cut the corroded pipes from the insides of the boilers with a blowtorch, then descaled the walls with a pneumatic chisel. He was surrounded by purple smoke and flying grit, and he came home at night with welts on his arms and back where flecks of hot metal had burned through his welder's smock.

At Papa Gino's on a Friday night in October, Dave Grobak's wife, Laura, told Ralph and Paula that the only reason she still had her job at InterBay Bank in New Haven was because she and Dave had a mortgage there. "They're cutting people right and left," she said, "but it's kind of an inside joke. They've got so many foreclosures they don't want to get rid of anybody who owes them money."

Ralph's sister, Mindy, had come to dinner, too, fresh from her first modelling job in six months—she had worn lingerie for a J. Wolf advertising supplement. Recounting her day, she said, "What I kept thinking about is these women's magazines. About ten times a year they have a story about 'A Day in the Life of a Model,' and the girl always says, 'It's not easy! It's hard work! I'm so bizzee!' Well, that's a lot of crap. I spent one day standing around and I made three hundred dollars. Those guys should try being waitresses."

"When're these pictures coming out?" Dave Grobak asked.

"Forget it."

"Lacroix's going to pass out copies," Ralph told him.

Lacroix was late. Eventually they saw his truck turning in to the lot. Despite the hour—it was almost dark—and the time of year, the restaurant's automatic sprinkler system was on. It drenched the small front lawn, the sidewalk, and part of the street, and Lacroix had to circle well out onto Sharpe Avenue as he came from the parking lot to the door.

"Ever since he got banged up he's completely irresponsible," Mindy grumbled. "He thinks he can turn up late—he thinks he can do anything he wants."

"Since?" Ralph asked. "He's always been that way."

Lacroix's leg was still intermittently inflamed, and often he had a mild cold. The hospital had done diagnostic tests, but the results were inconclusive. The drugs he received seemed to help, but when he stopped taking them the infection flared up again. Since he was still drawing compensation for the injury and had time on his hands, Ralph had talked him into taking fall courses at Southern Connecticut State University. Lacroix had gone to college for a couple of years before quitting to work construction, and Ralph thought going back would be good for him. He and Mindy were sharing rides to classes—over the last month, the two of them had split up and had gotten back together.

"I'm glad you guys patched it up," Ralph told her.

"Everybody thinks it's O.K. to just talk about us," Mindy announced. "It's like we're soap-opera characters."

"You said it," Paula told her.

"He apologized, O.K.? He always apologizes. He always says he's a terrible person and I shouldn't have anything to do with him, but he really likes me, so that's supposed to make everything O.K."

"Well, he's a nice guy," Ralph said.

"You know what it's like?" Mindy said. "It's like

that song they play on the oldies stations—'Don't know much about history, don't know much biology.' The singer says he doesn't know this and he doesn't know that, he can't do this and he can't do that, he's a complete loser. But then he says, 'I love you,' and the girl is supposed to fall into his arms. That's the stupidest song anybody ever wrote. Who'd fall in love with a guy like that?"

Lacroix had joined them by this time. He wore a red wool shirt that was sun-bleached pink in places. Grinning, he put his arm around Mindy, who threw it off. "Not only that, I'm unemployed," he said. "How about a kiss?"

"You're not unemployed," Ralph growled. "Jesus Christ. You're the only one still on the payroll, and you keep telling everyone you're unemployed."

"Sorry," Lacroix said.

"Those workmen's-comp premiums are expensive. Give me some credit."

When they had finished their pizzas and were saying goodbye in the parking lot, Laura Grobak told Ralph, "QualiTex is the sort of company that does O.K. in a recession. Their stuff goes for repairs and maintenance. You guys are in trouble, but what do you expect? Construction always gets murdered. But you should see the bank. They've got nobody to blame but themselves. You should see the commercial loans they made. If a chimpanzee came in they would have given him a million bucks."

Ralph started laughing. "I must be pretty bad," he told her. "They turned me down last spring."

"I just don't understand it," Laura said. "I mean, the InterBay guys are stupid. I can accept that. Fine. But look at New York. New York bankers are supposed to be smart, right? They made loans to Third World countries and got murdered. They made loans during the energy crisis and got murdered. They got into the leveraged-buyout business and got murdered. Now it's real estate. They lent money to Donald Trump. Would you lend money to Donald Trump?"

"Your wife thinks I'm worse than a chimpanzee," Ralph told Grobak.

"She's been talking about Donald Trump in her sleep," Grobak said. "I wake up in the middle of the night and she's yelling, 'Would you lend money to Donald Trump?' "

By mid-December, Lacroix was dead. He was killed when his pickup truck and a pizza-delivery car crashed into each other on Route 147, in Middlefield, about two in the morning. Police weren't sure who had strayed into whose lane. They said the other driver, also killed, was off duty and was on his way home from a Christmas party. Blood tests indicated that he had been slightly drunker than Lacroix. The impact threw the pizza sign from the roof of the car fifty feet into the woods.

The shock and disorientation caused by the accident were made somehow more acute for Lacroix's family and friends by the fact that his death had had nothing to do with his leg. That seemed bizarre and unfair—as if Lacroix had been looking in one direction and had been flattened from another. The swelling in his shin had gotten much worse the preceding week, and he had been hospitalized briefly, and his doctors had scheduled exploratory surgery.

"What the hell's going *on?*" Ralph bellowed after getting the news on the phone from Ramsey. "If some guy has cancer does he get blown up in a plane crash?"

He couldn't get over it. "When I used to tell these guys they'd be in prison or worse if it wasn't for me, I didn't mean him," he said as he got ready on the morning of the funeral, and Paula looked around to make sure Mindy was out of earshot. Mindy had broken up with Lacroix again, apparently permanently, in early November. But she was very upset and had spent the last two nights with Ralph and Paula. She ended up staying with them for a week.

"You better calm down about this, Ralph," Paula said. "You're going to drive yourself nuts. It's not exactly out of left field. He got drunk all the time. He drove like a maniac."

Heagan was at the funeral at St. Joseph's Church—the first time Ralph had seen him since the night of the layoffs, when Heagan had attacked Grobak for insulting J.F.K. Both Heagan and Ralph spoke at the service. They called Lacroix a good friend and a reliable employee.

"This is really bad," Ralph said afterward, in the parking lot.

"I'm kind of mad at myself," Heagan said. "I wouldn't tell this to anybody but you. I was in there and I was really upset, but then I was thinking about him pissing off the roof into Ramsey's hard hat. That time Ramsey went to get doughnuts and left it on the ground. I couldn't say that in a church."

"He almost got Cobie once," Ralph said.

Cobie was a loan officer from Home Dime who had started swinging by Cote Hill to see Ralph after Ralph, for obvious reasons, had stopped returning his phone calls. "The personal banker!" everyone would yell whenever Cobie showed up. "Personal banking at its best!"

Ralph and Heagan talked for half an hour, and then Heagan left for a job he'd found at a Mobil station and convenience store next to I-91, in Cromwell. He said he'd call. A month later he did phone; he said his pickup was being repaired downtown and he needed a ride home. Ralph and Mindy went to get him.

They ended up sitting in Ralph's Buick, outside Heagan's trailer. The ground was covered with slush the consistency of the pulverized-ice drinks sold by Quik-Mart in the summer, and it slid in gobs from three old motorcycles Heagan had bought and scavenged for parts. Heagan liked motorcycles almost as much as Mylicki did. Inside the trailer, Heagan's two Dobermans were barking. People who visited him generally stayed outside.

"I wasn't that mad the night I hit Grobak," he said. "I mean, I wasn't mad at Grobak. I was just mad. He was asking to get slugged, so I slugged him."

"Grobak doesn't work for us," Ralph said. "Hit him if you want. That doesn't mean you have to disappear for the next six months."

"I sort of disappeared because a lot of this mess is my fault," Heagan said.

"What? Grobak?"

"Nope. The elderly housing bid."

"No way."

"Listen," Heagan said. "The Housing Authority's always dealing with the building inspectors. Those guys know each other. The inspectors practically live in the housing projects. Every time there's a fire or somebody smashes his place up they're over there. I think they get slid a little extra to go easy on the code violations. So I nailed the plywood wrong and Magnin got mad, and what do you think happened? Magnin went and talked to the Housing Authority board. I heard about it. They could have given us the contract. They don't even like DeConcitti. But Magnin changed their minds. I saw him a few days after the plywood thing and he was telling me, 'You fuckers are going to be sorry.' "

"I still don't know if I believe that," Ralph said after a minute. "Maybe I should've bribed him, like everybody said. I always figured he was straight."

"He just had a good way to screw us over," Heagan said.

They were quiet for a minute, and then Ralph said, "We would have lasted a few more months. That's all. There's no work."

"That's what I don't understand," Mindy announced from the backseat. They'd almost forgotten she was there. "Why did you guys do this in the first place? You built the condos and half of 'em are empty. Everybody in town's mad at you, and you're broke. So why did you even start?"

"You typed two or three letters a week for me and made a hundred fifty bucks!" Ralph yelled. "Under the table! Tax-free! Now you're running down the construction business. Get out of the car! I don't want nothing to do with you."

Mindy stayed where she was. "Why did you do that with the plywood?" she asked Heagan.

"I hate the guy," Heagan said. He stared at the ceiling of the car and started to laugh. "I wanted to make him sweat a little when it wouldn't make any difference. Look what happened."

Ralph rubbed his forehead. "What difference *does* it make?" he asked.

"Well, what else are we going to do?" Heagan said. "What else is Mylicki going to do that pays him like that? He went all the way to Florida, and there was no work for him there, either, so now he's back."

"Maybe a month ago I would have thought this was a problem," Ralph said. "I remember thinking it would be a problem if Lacroix got better, because then I'd have to lay him off."

The dogs were barking again, and Heagan rolled his window down and yelled for them to shut up. "You always worried about him a lot," he said to Ralph. "Why did you do that?"

"I don't know," Ralph said. "He was like some little kid everybody took care of."

"Shut up!" Mindy shrieked. "You can't talk about him that way!"

She began to cry, and Ralph turned in his seat and said he was sorry.

In the middle of February, Ralph got a phone call from a cardiologist in New Haven, who said he was thinking about building a large house on four acres at the top of Cote Hill. Talking with this man, Ralph felt chilly around the neck and shoulders. The doctor didn't say he'd hire Bilt-Rite to build the house, and Ralph didn't say he wouldn't sell the land unless his company got the construction contract.

After hanging up, Ralph drove the flatbed truck downtown. He had to clear the company scaffolding out of the basement of his old office: someone was renting the space for warehousing. Ramsey and Mylicki were going to help him take the boards and pipes back to his house. Ralph got to the office first and waited in the truck in the parking lot. It was a little after ten in the morning. Clouds the color of foundry metal flew over the bricks. Winter had beaten the weeds and sumac along the railroad tracks down to a yellow stubble. There had been a pronounced cold snap—Ralph had spent several miserable days with his father thawing pipes in flooded basements—and now the temperature was hovering around freezing. The puddles in the parking lot turned blue whenever a patch of clear sky came overhead. Ralph felt hope bounding in his chest like a small animal. He aimed a wink at a picture of his sister pasted to the dashboard.

The J. Wolf advertising supplement featuring Mindy had come out the week before, and he and Ramsey and Mylicki had taped the photos of her all over the insides of their pickups. She had appeared in only three photographs, each a group shot.

Mindy was angry about being turned into a pinup

girl, and Ralph quickly took all his photos down except this one, above the heater-defrost control. In it, Mindy was wearing a plain-looking bra—no lace. She wasn't as pretty as the girl next to her.

Ramsey and Mylicki drove up in Ramsey's truck, and Ralph could hear them talking as they got out. "I took the pills, my blood pressure's down, and I'm better," Mylicki said. "It's simple."

"It doesn't work that way, stupid."

"That's what the clinic told me. Fuck them, too."

Ralph told them about the cardiologist. "Don't get too excited," he said. "He's probably called twenty other guys."

"That's good land, though," Mylicki said. "He's got a view there."

"He's got a view if he likes to look at Sharpe Avenue and the highways," Ralph said.

They carried planks and pipes out of the basement for forty-five minutes. Grobak, who was down there on some QualiTex business, quit what he was doing and helped them. He got dirt and grease all over his white shirt. He was Ramsey's new boss: Ramsey was sewing turbine covers for QualiTex now, and recently the company had hired him one day a week for warehouse work. Still, he was having trouble meeting his mortgage, and he seemed moody and depressed. After loading the scaffolding, they all threw a football around for a few minutes, and then Grobak left for lunch.

Ralph bounced up Raylene Drive in his truck, with stacks of scaffolding rattling in the back. He could see

Ramsey and Mylicki in the rearview mirror, in Ramsey's pickup. They were all headed for Ralph's house, where they were going to store the scaffolding for the time being. The house was three years old now, and Ralph still hadn't finished it. Like other small-time builders, he was busy with his customers when business was good, and he couldn't afford home-improvement projects when contracts were scarce. Raylene Drive, which was unpaved, had once served as a rear entrance to the Mohr traprock quarry, but the quarry's excavations had cut off the far end in the early seventies. What was left wound through some woods by a low ridge that overlooked a golf course and ended after a fifth of a mile at a clearing that once had held a small trailer park—housing, in the sixties, for seasonal quarry workers. Ralph owned two scrubby acres here—he hadn't gotten his grass in—flanked on the low side by an old rail line, where small trees grew between the tracks. A wooden bridge had been removed, but there was a footpath up the far side of the railroad cut, and the road beyond was lined with old trucks and boilers and gravel-crushing equipment. The week after he closed the company, Ralph had spent a lot of time out there, trying to calm down.

He and Heagan had poured the concrete for the garage floor when they put in the foundation of the house. The unfinished garage had become an informal patio, and during the happy summers of the construction boom the crew had come over for dinner once or twice a week, and Ralph had barbecued chicken for them in a sawed-off barrel. Now he and Mylicki and Ramsey began to pile Bilt-Rite's scaffolding on the concrete. It was a gritty winter day, and as Ralph slogged over the half-frozen ground, carrying pieces of his dismantled business, he felt depression dropping around him like a curtain. This was hard work, and he usually associated scaffolding—whether going up or down—with the cheerful activities of construction and money-making. Piling it here, when the reason was his own insolvency, he found it hard to believe that a cardiologist would hire him to build a three-hundred-thousand-dollar house.

They had to walk the last ten yards, because the driveway was gravelled only to the point where the front walk hooked in. The final stretch was uphill, and Ralph didn't want to risk the truck in the mud and ice. Past the corner of the house, the construction forklift, wrapped in green tarps, poked dinosaurlike into the air. The nail guns and air compressors had been put away in the cellar.

After twenty minutes, Ralph heard boards shifting and Ramsey yelling as he slipped. As Ramsey went down, one of the planks hit him in the face. His nose was bleeding and he seemed dizzy as they helped him inside. Paula, who had come home for lunch, went to the refrigerator for an ice pack. Ralph and Mylicki went back outside after a few minutes, leaving Ramsey in the kitchen. His clothes were covered with mud, and so was the kitchen floor.

Ralph himself slipped ten or fifteen minutes later— in the shadowy spots, the ground was frozen beneath a slick surface of mud. They were finished with the planks and had started with the pipes. He was carrying three of them, and he threw them to his right as he fell, and ended up on his forearms and knees. Muddy water splashed onto his face and chest, and the cold shocked him. Just below the water, the ground was as hard as concrete.

When Ralph and Mylicki were done, they slogged up the steps to the kitchen door. As Ralph opened it, he heard Ramsey, extremely upset, telling Paula, "It's simple! There's a recession, people need jobs, they should make some goddam jobs!"

"Your boots!" Paula shrieked, because Ralph had continued directly into the kitchen. She had just cleaned up Ramsey's mess.

"It's like that stuff with Lacroix's leg," Ramsey said. His nose had stopped bleeding, but his voice was hoarse. "What's the big deal? There's something wrong, they're the fucking doctors, why didn't they fix it? What's the problem? Maybe if they'd fixed his leg, he wouldn't have crashed."

"What are you talking about?" Paula said, staring at him.

Ralph went to the counter by the sink and took the pot from the coffeemaker and a mug from the cupboard. "I must be stupid," he said as he sat down. "I don't understand anything that's happened the last six months, but everybody else around here always says everything's simple. We don't know why the lumber blew up on Lacroix in the first place, right? But don't mind me. Everything's simple."

"Clean off your face and change your clothes," Paula told him. When he ignored her, she got up, took her coat from the hook, and left.

Ramsey had removed his jacket. Ralph, who wasn't

injured, only dirty, hadn't even taken off his work gloves. They were soaked with mud, and his coat sleeves left vague brown swirls, like something done with watercolor, on the yellow Formica of the table. A streak of dirt ran across his forehead. He was slumped in his chair. "I guess she's going back to work," he said. "So what's simple? Tell me one thing that's simple around here."

Mylicki, coming in, said, "Ramsey has to think that way. He's a moron."

"You're both morons," Ralph said angrily. "I bet this is why the Japs are taking over the country. You think they think things are simple? You think the Germans think things are simple? You think they have recessions over there because people are so stupid they lend money to Donald Trump?"

"What?" Ramsey asked.

Mylicki started to laugh. "When they take over the country, they can put me and Ramsey in a zoo," he said. "Everybody else can come and look."

"Why don't you guys get out of here?" Ralph said. He propped his face in his muddy palms. "Thanks for the help and get the hell out of here."

After they were gone, he sat there for several minutes, then stood up and tried to throw his coffee cup through the kitchen window. The window had a number of small panes, and the cup hit one of the interior frames, cracking the adjacent glass, fell back into the kitchen, and shattered in the sink. Then Ralph raked his chair over the counter, sweeping the other cups onto the floor. After that, he slammed the chair onto the table. The chair didn't break, although one of its legs was bent. Panting, he put the chair upright and sat down again.

Heagan showed up twenty minutes later. Ralph hadn't cleaned the place and hadn't changed his clothes. He seemed calm enough. After letting Heagan in the kitchen door, he crunched over the broken cups to his place at the table.

"News travels," Heagan said. "I just saw Grobak at McDonald's. Who's the rich guy that wants a house?"

"You and Grobak are talking to each other now?"

"That fight was months ago. Sure."

"I just told Ramsey and Mylicki to get out of here. They were driving me nuts."

Heagan was looking around the kitchen.

"Things are so bad I can't even get mad anymore," Ralph explained. "I started doing this and I kept thinking I should stop."

"You cleaning this up before Paula gets home?"

"I'm trying to think of something to do where I'll respect myself. I haven't thought of it yet."

"Clean it up, you jerk. Don't get her mad."

"This team is wrecked," Ralph said. "Lacroix's dead, and those guys are a couple of babies. How'd I get into this mess? I got half my stuff sitting outside in the middle of winter."

"Have you called this rich guy back yet?"

"He just called this morning."

"Don't give me any team stuff right now," Heagan said. "Don't get mushy. This is business."

Ralph went to the refrigerator and got Heagan a beer, then indicated a rocking chair that was just inside the living-room doorway. Strangely enough, the chair had been the cause of Heagan's fight with Dave Grobak back in August. Paula had ordered it from L. L. Bean— practically the only thing she and Ralph had ever gotten from a catalogue.

"Uh-oh," Heagan said now, dragging the rocker into the kitchen. He sat in it and smiled. The chair had been on the patio the night of the layoffs, and Grobak had recognized it as an L. L. Bean Presidential Rocker. Grobak also had remembered that the catalogue said the rocker was the kind J.F.K. had used to relieve his lower-back pain. Grobak had asked if there was also an "L. L. Bean Presidential Adultery Mattress" on which Kennedy had gotten the back pain to begin with. There was a big mess after that—Heagan all over Grobak, who was half his size, three or four others struggling to pull Heagan off, people yelling, beer bottles falling from the picnic table and exploding on the concrete. Lacroix banged his leg again.

"I almost wish Grobak didn't tell me about this house," Heagan said to Ralph. "Now he's got me thinking about it."

"I'm thinking about last week," Ralph said. "I did five or six flooded basements with Rollo. You know what that's like. I kept telling myself, 'Never again,' and that's dangerous. I could be out there next week. We don't know what's going to happen with anything right now."

For years, Rollo had wanted help during cold snaps, and for years Ralph had managed to be too busy. "We were driving home," he told Heagan, "and I said to Rollo, 'This is terrible. My company's gone.' And

Rollo said, 'I've been in wet cellars my whole life, and you do it one day and you turn into a goddam baby. Shut up.' That was the worst, when he said that."

Ralph had been grouchy about thawing the pipes, although he was grateful for the money. "It's purple out," he'd said to Rollo, with disgust, as they were carting their equipment up the back steps and out to Rollo's van. Their feet were frozen, the tips of the trees were bare, and there were steely patches of ice here and there in the grass.

"I sort of understand why you hit Grobak," he told Heagan. "I was surprised at first, but I've been thinking about it."

Heagan said, "Somebody messes with J.F.K., I'm going to bust his nose. I don't care if the guy was thirty years ago."

"It's like having your childhood insulted," Ralph said. Mention of J.F.K. made him think of small ranch houses, Ford Fairlanes baking in driveways, and circular backyard swimming pools with mothers sitting around in lawn chairs, smoking cigarettes and talking about Jackie. In the house he'd grown up in on Kati Lane, his father, an ex-Navy man, had kept a model of the U.S.S. Missouri in the bedroom. "Rollo and my mother thought things were O.K. there for a while," Ralph said. "They had a Catholic President in the White House and the Singing Nun on the radio. I think Rollo even went to church a few times."

Ralph and Heagan were the same age, and both had grown up in subdivisions filled with the kind of houses they later built. Heagan sometimes said construction was like being a kid—you spent all day playing in the dirt, swearing, and making noise with your friends. "The Singing Nun committed suicide," he said now. "That's what I heard."

"What did your parents think when they found out Kennedy messed around?" Ralph asked. "That he did it right in the White House?"

"I don't know. I never asked them about it."

When Heagan got up to go a few minutes later, Ralph went along as far as the walk. The weather had closed in and snow was starting to fall.

"I'll call the doctor about the house in a couple of days," Ralph said. "I don't want to push too hard too fast."

"Whatever," Heagan said. He hoisted himself into his pickup with a construction-worker's move, hauling with both hands from above and swinging his feet into the cab. He stuck his head out the window as he backed down the drive.

Ralph watched the pickup go up the road. It dimmed and then disappeared in the descending gray flakes. He found himself wondering what was so bad about calling themselves a team. As soon as the company had fallen apart, everybody started getting into trouble. At least when Bilt-Rite was on a job, things never got completely out of hand. But Heagan thought all this was mushy, and so would Rollo if Ralph was ever foolish enough to bring it up. It bothered Ralph that he was less tough than his father. Rollo didn't even think that what Ralph was going through right now was a very hard time. Ralph shrugged, giving it up, and went inside to clean up the kitchen.

Airport Beach

Z ANSKE, the attendance officer responsible for the high school, came to work on Senior Skip Day and found a letter from the superintendent of schools in his mail cubbyhole. It congratulated him for twenty years' of service as a truant officer and regretted that two weeks ago he had been involved in an "unfortunate incident while on the job."

That was a reference to May 12th, when Zanske had been stabbed in the stomach by a nine-year-old girl named Lucia Ramos. Zanske had gone to Lucia's mother's apartment at the Kennedy public-housing project to see why the girl had been absent for three days in a row—the twenty-ninth, thirtieth, and thirty-first days she had missed since September. Lucia was a student at Braddock Elementary, one of three elementary schools Zanske dealt with along with the high school. Lucia hadn't seemed angry or frightened when she had closed the door in Zanske's face, and he had assumed that she was taking the chain off. He started forward as it began to open again, but the chain was still on, and extending through the gap was Lucia's thin hand, holding a small kitchen knife. Zanske walked into the knife—he more or less impaled himself. It wasn't clear that Lucia had intended to stab him; she might only have wanted him to go away.

The wound wasn't serious, because the knife had a short blade and because Zanske weighed close to three hundred pounds. An intern at the hospital explained that Zanske had an unusually thick layer of adipose tissue, the lining of fat directly under the skin of the stomach. There were few nerves there, and the blood vessels were small. The fat itself was yellow and ugly. (Zanske saw it when the wound was cleaned out.) The knife hadn't gotten through this barrier to the intestinal wall. Zanske received six stitches.

The police reported that Lucia Ramos's mother's boyfriend had told the girl that everyone in the family would go to jail if she let a stranger into the apartment. The mother came home at nine that evening and was arrested on charges of possessing unregistered weapons when she couldn't find permits for two pistols found lying on top of the refrigerator. Detectives were still searching for the boyfriend, who had been sentenced in October to two years for selling cocaine but had been let out after three months. Zanske didn't return to work until the following morning. He could have gone straight from the hospital, but he saw no glory in being stabbed by a nine-year-old girl, or in avoiding serious injury as he had avoided it. He knew that because the police were involved, and because the matter was work-related, the Guidance Department and the superintendent's office would be notified, and shortly after that everyone at the high school would know all about it.

Zanske reviewed the attendance sheets at the large table in the center of the guidance office, occasionally coming up for air, sometimes fastening his gaze on the front page of the local paper from two days ago, which had been pinned to the bulletin board. It quoted the president of the Taxpayer League—who, it could be seen from the photograph, wasn't a small woman—using the refrain "What about the little people?" several times before the City Council as she was complaining about the size of next year's school budget and the level of teachers' salaries. It wasn't the sort of thing that would make her popular around here—there had been layoffs at the high school last September—and someone had underlined the word "little" with a red felt-tip pen and had added three question marks and an arrow pointed at her torso. Someone else had drawn a bone through her head. It was unusual to have staff commentary like that displayed in a room used by students.

It turned out that seven hundred and two of the high school's twelve hundred and seventy-three students were absent. That was a record, but not a surprise. The temperature this week had reached eighty for the first time since last September, the end of classes was approaching, and Senior Skip Day, which was celebrated each year on the Friday before Memorial Day weekend, was more popular every year.

Zanske went off to see Chuck Dankilow, the principal, anticipating a trip to Airport Beach, where he might come across a small portion of this missing crowd. Airport Beach was a strip of sand by the chain-link fence at the southern end of the regional airport. Planes—single-engine Cessnas and occasional corporate jets—came directly overhead. There was no water, but there was an open horizon, and high-school kids gathered there. In the summer, a van parked in the dust, and a couple in their sixties sold hot dogs from a window in its side.

Zanske went to Airport Beach officially and unofficially. He and Gary Scottnicki, who managed a QuikMart on Sharpe Avenue, had a habit of sitting there at night, in Zanske's Pontiac Grand Prix, and drinking beer. The Pontiac had been built before cars were downsized, and the front seat was more or less a portable couch. Zanske had frequented Airport Beach and other scruffy, informal gathering spots—litter-festooned, bottle-strewn, urine-redolent—when he was a teenager, and simply hadn't stopped. There was an overlook by the Connecticut River, a pull-off by the ninth hole of the golf course, fronted by a graffiti-covered stone fence, and a dam at the former Meaponk Reservoir. The kids knew who Zanske was; if he ran into truants late at night, when he was off duty, he often pointed out (while hiding his beer) that he couldn't help it if his eyes were open.

Truant officers didn't drag anyone to school anymore, and their rules of operation—at least around here—were vague. They held meetings with parents; they talked to the absentees about what was troubling them. Not much seemed to work. One thing that didn't was counselling. Kids who would rather be absent from school certainly preferred being absent from these appointments to being branded defective in some way, and so they failed to show up for the diagnostic tests and the sessions with the psychologists even more obstinately than they failed to show up for class. Zanske tried to enroll persistent offenders in the alternate school, but the alternate school was overcrowded and its director usually sent them back, claiming that youngsters with attendance difficulties didn't do well in an "unstructured setting." Zanske supposed it was important for an attendance officer to be seen around town by high-school kids, and to know what was going on with them, but he might have supposed this because he loitered in these places anyway and was seen by them as a matter of course.

This morning Dankilow surprised him by telling him to go to Hammonasset Beach, on Long Island Sound. Hammonasset was the destination of choice on Senior Skip Day (the airport was for less exalted holidays), and in fact twenty-five years ago Zanske had gone there himself. But Hammonasset also was thirty miles away. Zanske usually stayed within the city limits, and it seemed to him that he had little enough power there. He had no idea what he was supposed to accomplish at a state park in a different county.

"I know I'm not supposed to get mad about half the school taking the day off," Dankilow said. He was clearly furious.

"I got no jurisdiction there," Zanske grumbled. "What do you want me to do? Chase 'em all over the beach?"

"I catch so much hell for this every year,"

Dankilow said. He meant from the school superintendent. Last week he and Superintendent Harold Petrosky
had mailed a form letter to parents explaining that Senior Skip Day wasn't "approved or condoned by the
high school or the Education Department."

"If you'd told me yesterday, I could've been at Mc-
Donald's at seven-thirty this morning," Zanske said.
"That's where they meet. These kids aren't the problem
anyway. It's the kids who skip when it isn't Skip Day."

"You're the one who doesn't understand the problem," Dankilow told him, glaring. "I've got to do
something just to say I'm doing something. Get down
there, tell 'em they've get fifteen detentions each, tell
'em the senior outing's cancelled."

There was no point to any of this. The students
knew they'd get the detentions, assuming they didn't
come up with contrived excuses signed by their parents.
The rule was three after-school periods per class missed,
and there were five classes each day. The kids would be
staying after school for three weeks, except most
wouldn't stay. That would be followed by the usual
threat about seniors not being allowed to graduate because detentions were outstanding. The parents always
got too upset about that for Dankilow to make it stick.
As for the senior outing—softball, volleyball, and a barbecue at Cliffside Meadows, in Portland—that had been
cancelled for four years running. Each time, the senior
class had forfeited the five-hundred-dollar deposit put
down to reserve the pavilion-restaurant. Cliffside
bought a roast beef each year—the size of a stuffed
chair. Zanske wondered what happened to it.

"I didn't see Rascati on that list," Dankilow said.

"He's on it."

It irked Dankilow that Senior Skip Day was observed by so many underclassmen, and especially by underclassmen like Rascati. Two weeks ago, Rascati, a sophomore, had been arrested on charges of burglary and possession of an unregistered weapon—"extracurricular sports," the staff called it, because it had nothing to do with school. It wasn't clear what would happen with all that—the affair was shrouded in the workings of the juvenile court. Then, last week, Rascati had been suspended from school for two days because he had showed up, for a change, and had casually disrupted the National Honor Society assembly. At the assembly, Rascati had begun a whispered chant, which spread until the auditorium sounded as if it were full of snakes. The school's brightest students had mounted the stage accompanied by the word "nerds," hissed repeatedly, with the "s" drawn out.

Zanske thought that suspending habitual truants for things they did when they actually came to class was a bad idea, but in this case Dankilow wouldn't back down. Dankilow stubbornly maintained that a good education could be got here by anyone who cared to try, and he couldn't stand to see the better students mocked. Anyone who was even slightly serious about studying was sequestered in honors classes as early as freshman year, as a form of protection—most of the nation's problems seemed to be crammed into the school's hallways. The city, which was large enough to have a sizable minority population, a slum area, a serious drug trade, and surprisingly good traffic jams, also was small enough to have failed to spill out into suburban communities. Kids from outlying neighborhoods whose parents had white-collar jobs in Hartford and New Haven were on the same teams and in some of the same classes as kids from the downtown housing projects. The older ethnic neighborhoods in town—Polish, Italian, French—were decaying somewhat and losing families to the subdivisions, but they still held many well-maintained two- and three-family houses, where parents expected the graduates of the parochial elementary schools to get good grades at West High. Two students from Dankilow's school had gone to Dartmouth last year, and two had been indicted for murder.

Rascati was olive-skinned, medium-size, and fully fleshed. His mother was either Korean or Japanese. He sometimes called Zanske late at night, although Zanske's home number was unlisted. The phone would ring at three in the morning and Rascati would ask, "Hey, Fuckface! Do blimps sleep?" Or he'd say he was in Middletown and needed a ride home. "This is your big chance—only time you'll ever catch me."

"Shut the hell up."

"Hey! There's a full moon! You sticking your ass out the window again?"

Rascati made Zanske think of some plump-cheeked Asian gangster, although he had nothing against the local Asians. Two of the last three valedictorians had been Pakistani immigrants who had grown up in the Kennedy public-housing project, and last month a Cambodian boy at Braddock Elementary had won the citywide spelling bee, unseating a long line of eleven-year-old parochial-school girls. The kid had won even though he hadn't spoken English until he was six. Each year a few students from the housing projects made it to college, and each year Dankilow held a banquet for the top twenty students in each class. He thought they deserved a celebration of the sort thrown by parents' booster clubs for the football and basketball teams. He was fiercely protective of the National Honor Society.

Zanske didn't remind Dankilow that a good percentage of the National Honor Society was at the beach today. Dankilow knew; he had been principal for six years.

Not many of the high-school teachers had ever been elected to the National Honor Society. Most had gotten B's and C's and had gone to the regional state universities—the teacher factories. They weren't thrilled with the National Honor Society ceremony or with the ridiculous, awkward tea party that followed it. They found Rascati amusing, on the other hand, and frequently talked about whether or not he would impregnate Diane Trella or Mary Juventus, sophomores who were referred to in the faculty room as "princesses" or "Barbies"—teacher slang for girls who were well turned-out, got good grades, and had high opinions of themselves. These two were blonde and wore clothes that were somewhat on the prim side of fashionable. Rascati, meanwhile, was an example of what the teachers called "the leader-of-the-pack syndrome." He appealed to girls who shouldn't go anywhere near him.

As Zanske left school around nine-thirty, he was

surprised to see Mary Juventus at her locker, and he stopped and stared at her for a moment.

"What?" she said sulkily. "I didn't do anything."

"Nope," he said. "Absolutely not. Well, well, well." He went on down the hall, wondering whether her presence in school on Senior Skip Day made her less of a princess or more of one.

At Braddock Elementary, half a mile away and that much closer to the downtown, Zanske panted up the front steps and hoped he wouldn't run into Lucia Ramos in the hall. That had happened twice since the stabbing. Each time Lucia had fled in tears. After the second incident, Lucia's school psychologist had called Zanske and complained.

"Try to leave her alone, will you?" she asked.

"What makes you think I want to see her?" Zanske bellowed.

"Try a little harder. I don't want her getting upset. She just moved in with her grandmother and it seems to be working out."

"Give me a break," Zanske said. "That'll last about a week."

When Zanske got to the office today, he found there was no danger of running into Lucia—she was absent again. The principal wasn't at his desk, and Zanske sat in the orange plastic chair set aside for visitors and scanned the rest of the attendance report. The Gates boys had missed the whole week—Darryl Gates, second grade, and Pernell, fourth grade. They made Zanske nervous, because they always looked at him as if they wanted to see something impressive in this huge adult who sometimes paid attention to them. Zanske had gone by their apartment on Tuesday—door locked, no one home. A social worker had visited last week and found trash on the floor and maggots crawling over a hot plate. The mother had explained that she was having trouble with her welfare payments, and that the electricity had been turned off. "Maggots on a hot plate" had become a phrase Zanske sometimes repeated to himself, along with "sick puppy"—a term he frequently used in talking to the students, much as he might have called them "bub," or "pal."

When Larry Schulberg, Braddock's principal, came in a few minutes later, he was grinning. He handed Zanske a sheet of yellow construction paper. Drawn on it was a jet, with apples and oranges scrawled on the wings and fuselage and bananas in the windows. It was signed "Joey W." Darla Mancini's fourth-grade class had been illustrating verses from "America the Beautiful," and this was Joey Ward's version of the "fruited plain."

"Darla wants to make fruited-plane hats for the end-of-the-year assembly," Schulberg said. "I told her the superintendent's office'd kill me."

On the last day of school each year, the students at Braddock held a party in the cafeteria. They wore paper hats they had made—each class chose a different theme. It was a colorful sight, and there was a sound system set up for dancing. Everyone seemed to have a good time.

Zanske said, "I got a letter from the superintendent right here," and pulled it from his sport coat pocket.

"I like his way with words," Schulberg said after a

minute. "I really do. 'Unfortunate incident while on the job.' If I get killed driving home tonight, will he send a card to my wife about my 'unfortunate incident while on the highway'?"

Zanske left a few minutes later and drove to the Gates boys' apartment. It was on the first floor of a two-family house on Loudner Street. No one was home, and a large pink eviction notice had been nailed to one of the posts of the front porch.

Hammonasset was a forty-minute trip, a lot of it on Route 79 through countryside that was rural for Connecticut, which meant that there were small houses—capes and split-levels—by the road, but woods on the hills beyond. Sand from the winter lined the edges of the asphalt and was almost white in the sun. Zanske could smell warm earth through the open window of his car.

The attendant at the beach's Hansel-and-Gretel gatehouse let him past without charge when he said he was a school official. "You better hurry," she said. "I think they're closing the place down."

The vast parking lots were about half full. It was almost noon, and Zanske knew that many of the kids would be gone already. After three or four hours they had usually had enough sun and beer and were ready for a shower and a nap. He found a parking place in the front lot and went across the wooden pavilion by the snack bar and onto the low boardwalk. He felt foolish in his jacket and tie. He had told Dankilow he wasn't going to walk in the sand—you couldn't do that comfortably in shoes, and he certainly wasn't taking his off. Any looking around and any negotiating would take place from the boardwalk.

It was a long beach and he wondered how he would find anyone, but almost immediately Rudy D'Angelo and Mark Spaginsky came out of the snack bar.

"Jesus Christ!" Rudy yelled, flinging down a half-consumed cigarette. It was an odd reflex. Clearly, the teachers who patrolled the men's room had surprised Rudy a few times. Spaginsky, on the other hand, didn't seem to be drunk.

"Will you relax?" Zanske said. "You think I'm going to arrest five hundred people?"

"How many skipped?" Rudy asked.

Zanske, lying easily, said they hadn't set any records. Meanwhile he gazed at the beach. Park rangers stood at intervals along the shoreline. Small knots of teenagers in bathing suits were peering past them into the water, and others were gathering their towels and suntan lotion into beach bags.

"The ocean's got garbage in it," Spaginsky said. "They want everybody to go. They won't even feed us in the snack bar. A couple hours ago they were looking in coolers and taking everybody's beer. It's like they're daring you to have a good time."

"They probably put the garbage in the water on purpose," D'Angelo said.

Zanske got some reluctant directions from them and found the main encampment from the high school after a three-minute stroll to the east. Students came to

Hammonasset from all over the state on Senior Skip Day, but as far as Zanske could tell they didn't mix much from school to school. He was greeted with shrieks and cheers, and several of the girls, as if they were embarrassed to be seen wearing bathing suits, covered themselves with towels. Diane Trella pulled on a T-shirt and pants, either because Zanske had arrived or because a park ranger was pestering everyone to leave. It was a pale to sunburned crowd; Zanske didn't see any of the school's black or Hispanic students. The waves were low and the water a grayish brown, and there was a plane droning overhead. He heard Tricia Morjassian telling the ranger that a shredded plastic garbage bag had wrapped around her leg while she was wading. "There was scuzz all over it," she said.

Several of the boys began to yell, saying they weren't going to leave, and after a minute Dave Sappman came over to Zanske and asked, "You taking our names down?"

"Don't need to take your names down, Sick Puppy," Zanske said. "You're already on the list. I just came to say hi."

"We shouldn't get in trouble over this. It wasn't even worth it."

"You think this is trouble?" Zanske asked. "This prissy little party you're having?"

Zanske hadn't seen Rascati, but at the Wendy's on Route 1, where he bought the New Haven newspaper from a box in the parking lot and then wedged himself into the cattle pen leading to the counter, he ran into Spaginsky and D'Angelo again. He said to Spaginsky, "You're driving, right? Rudy's too plowed."

The restaurant was glutted with teenagers evacuated from the beach. "Damn right he's driving," D'Angelo said. "Spags is my slave. Pick my nose, Spags."

"You're walking," Spaginsky told him. He explained to Zanske that he had borrowed his father's car from the commuter lot by I-91. It had to be back by five—in the same parking space or one near enough that his father wouldn't know the difference. While Spaginsky talked, Rudy drank mechanically from a half-gallon ginger-ale bottle made of green plastic. Apparently that was how he'd fooled the rangers, although Zanske wondered what four or five cans' worth of warm beer would taste like after sloshing around in plastic for several hours. He said, "You guys better enjoy yourselves. You're going to be paying for this a long time."

"He's right," Rudy said. "We should be having more fun than this. We should've gone to Cape Cod."

"I think there are some batting machines around here," Zanske said.

He looked at the two of them—Rudy was flushed and weaving slightly on his feet—and considered how it would feel to drive to the beach with a bunch of friends only to find garbage in the water and park rangers ransacking coolers and duffel bags. The prospects hadn't been so dim on his own Senior Skip Day, although he'd had other problems, such as being too fat to be seen in a bathing suit. He'd spent all day in the parking lot, leaning on fenders and smoking cigarettes. Back then, Zanske's concept of the beach hadn't required an ocean; the beach was just another place you went to hang around with your car. He hadn't gotten close enough to see Long Island Sound that day.

Today's problem with the garbage wasn't much of a surprise. Over the past few years, the park had been closed several times for this reason, and there had been wide TV and newspaper coverage. Swimming in Long Island Sound wasn't as popular as it used to be, but still, Zanske supposed, among teenagers there was a tendency to think that certain days and certain traditions were sacred.

"Dankilow cancelled the senior outing," he told Dave McCauley, who was standing ahead of him in line.

"Whoopie shit," McCauley said.

McCauley, D'Angelo, and the several others began to talk of going on to Misquamicut, in Rhode Island, but Zanske didn't think they'd get there. The kids would filter home, and a good portion of them would show up at the mall in a few hours. Once it was dark, they'd disperse to the archipelago of local hanging-around places—the airport, the Connecticut River overlook, the Meaponk Dam.

A few minutes later he took his cheeseburger and the newspaper out to the car. On the front page an article reported that fifty homeowners had complained about the smell coming from a sewage-treatment plant. One of them, delivering a petition to City Hall, had claimed, "It's always the little people who get stuck with this stuff. Why don't they put it in someone else's neighborhood?" Zanske put down the paper for a moment. Thinking of the article posted in the guidance office, he wondered when the term "little people" had become so popular. It seemed odd that it was now fashionable around here for citizens to announce in public— and to announce almost proudly—that they were small and powerless.

When he got back to town, he drove past the high school without stopping, and a few minutes later turned in at the QuikMart, where his friend Gary Scottnicki was manager.

"I'm sick of this," he said, buying cigarettes. "If Dankilow's going to send me all over the place for no good reason, I'm going to go some place I feel like going. I'm driving up to Bradley. See if any of the little scuzzballs are up there, except they won't be."

Bradley was Bradley International Airport. Zanske felt like drinking a few beers, and if he took a six-pack to the regional airport while he was on duty, someone would see him.

"I'm knifeproof and everything," he told Scottnicki, "but three and a half inches of fat don't keep my ass out of trouble if I get caught goofing off."

Zanske liked Bradley anyway; there was a pull-off much like the one at Airport Beach, but there were bigger planes to watch and they took off and landed more frequently. It was shortly after two o'clock. He was supposed to work at least until four-thirty, but he had no afternoon conferences scheduled—truants and their parents were rarely available for meetings, and never on Friday afternoons before holiday weekends.

As he paid for the cigarettes, he told Scottnicki about Joey Ward's "fruited plane" drawing.

"The only fruit that kid sees is in the supermarket," Scottnicki said. "What do you expect?" He wore jeans and a yellow T-shirt and had a beard that needed trimming.

"You're cheerful today," Zanske said.

Scottnicki looked somewhere between irritable and ready for a nap. "When things suck, they suck," he said idly, sitting down behind the counter. He didn't like his job but hadn't been able to find anything else. He was older than Zanske—in his mid-forties.

They talked for a few minutes, and because there was no one else in the store Scottnicki followed Zanske out to the parking lot. They stood in the sun and lit cigarettes. The light banged off the stuccoed side of the building. Beyond the lot to the rear, before a subdivision began, was a small field with a flatbed trailer rusting in the middle of it. Again Zanske caught the scent of warm earth. He remembered having thought there was something promising about the smell when he was younger.

Smith Brothers Pizza was largely a take-out place, but there were two tables by the door, and Zanske had found it was useless to call ahead on Friday nights, because the phone was always busy. Once the orders piled up, the employees, no matter how angry it made potential customers, simply took the phone off the hook. Zanske had pizza from Smith Brothers three or four times a week, and little tolerance for busy signals when he was hungry. After finishing his six-pack at Bradley International, he showed up in person around seven-thirty, ate his dinner, then went home and showered and changed his clothes. At nine he went to Airport Beach.

There, much later, he saw Rascati. It was around midnight. Scottnicki had just pulled up in his pickup next to Zanske's Grand Prix. He had closed the store at eleven. Rascati was walking along the fence directly in front of them. It was essentially his shape that Zanske recognized, but then he got a flicker of the face in a turning headlight. Apparently the boy was coming from the far end of Airport Beach, where a clump of low trees served as a men's room. Zanske heard a car spinning its wheels down there, then hit his horn and made Rascati jump. "What is it with you?" he said, sticking his head out the window. "Everybody else goes to Hammonasset and you can't even get out of town?"

Rascati came forward, staring intently until he recognized who was talking to him. He was silhouetted against the spotlight attached to the nearest hangar. He paused to wipe his face with a sleeve, and asked, "You working now?"

"I don't know. Might be. Might not. It's hard to tell."

"What're you doing here?"

Zanske turned to Scottnicki and asked, "Why do they always think they own these places?"

They'd seen each other here once or twice, although Rascati didn't come that often. Rascati commented, "I heard some girl stuck you, but you didn't pop."

Zanske started to laugh. "You got problems of

your own. Seven hundred kids skipped today, and the only one the principal asked about was you. Maybe you better not come back. Were you planning on coming back before the end of the year?"

Rascati leaned against the fender of Zanske's car. Zanske decided he'd been drinking. "I don't know," Rascati told him. "It'd help if they sent somebody after me who didn't look like a giant pig." He wiped his face again, then lit a cigarette. "Give me a beer and I'll think about it."

Zanske was out of the car now, standing and resting his forearms on the open door. He reached in and put his beer on the dashboard. "Let me ask you something," he said. "You know what the fruited plain is?"

"You serious?"

Rascati seemed distracted. He was wiping his face and looking off to the left, in the direction he'd been walking when Zanske interrupted him. Zanske noticed a girl coming along the fence. Probably she had gotten tired of waiting in the car for Rascati to return. Then Zanske thought, What car? Rascati wasn't old enough to drive.

"I'm getting my hands on this tasty fruit over here," the boy said, standing up.

"Shut up," the girl told him.

Zanske thought he recognized Mary Juventus. "She's out with *you?*" he asked. Mary, recognizing Zanske, said *"God!"* with obvious disgust, and started away. Rascati called after her, "Wait a second."

Mary wheeled and yelled, "It's like having this huge pervert following you around! He's always looking at me!"

106

"Wait!" Rascati said.

"You forgot to say I'm fat and ugly," Zanske pointed out equably.

Mary ignored him. She came closer, put her hand over her mouth, then turned and ran away.

"I need some help," Rascati called to her, but Mary didn't hear him—she was fleeing down the dark line of cars.

"She's still getting used to all this stuff," Rascati explained. "Sex and so on. She thinks everybody can figure out what's going on just by seeing her."

Zanske came around the car door and asked, "What's wrong with you?"

Rascati was bleeding from the nose and mouth. From this angle, the blood glinted on his chin, and Zanske could see a large dark area on the front of his shirt.

"Can I have a beer?"

"Somebody beat you up?"

"When you try to fence stuff," Rascati told him, as if lecturing an idiot, "sometimes they rob you. If I had my gun this wouldn't have happened."

The gun, Zanske knew, had been confiscated at the time of the burglary charges. Police had found a pistol in Rascati's bedroom. The boy raised a hand, palm up. "I probably shouldn't get blood on her father's car," he said.

"Fuckin' A. You already dragged her in over her head."

"Naw. She was just along. She didn't know about this."

Scottnicki was dispatched—a slightly confused

107

emissary—to tell Mary Juventus to drive herself home. He came back and said, "Mary don't know how to drive."

Rascati was sitting in Zanske's passenger seat now, tending his nose with a balled-up napkin from an old fast-food bag that had been lying in Zanske's car. The napkin wasn't doing much to stop the bleeding.

"You stole the car?" Zanske yelled.

"I was with Mary," Rascati told him. "It's her parents' car. She said O.K. Who's stealing?"

Dankilow called at nine-thirty Saturday morning. "I've been trying to find you since one yesterday afternoon," he said. He explained that the guidance director had complained that Zanske hadn't followed up on seventeen recent referrals, all of them involving girls. "I was starting to get worried. You weren't in the office, you weren't home, you didn't leave any messages."

"Nope."

"What'd you do yesterday?"

"What do you think? I chased the little sick puppies around the beach."

"What happened?"

"Chuck, it was crazy. They knew I couldn't do anything. What was I going to say? The only one who was worried was Sappman, and he's a goddam baby. But you ought to feel pretty good. They closed the beach down—there was garbage in the water. Those kids didn't have any fun at all."

"You spent the whole day down there?"

"Naw. I went to Bradley International."

"The kids go up there now?"

"No," Zanske said. "But *I* had a good time."

"What's this stuff about the girls?"

"The guy's basically right. I haven't followed up on a girl in about three weeks. It's sort of getting to be a problem. I'm having trouble with the housing projects, too, and I should be spending a lot of time there. But I think I'm getting a handle on that."

"This isn't surprising, considering what happened," Dankilow said after a minute. "I don't think anybody expected you to be a hundred percent. I just wish you'd told me."

"I'm working on it."

"Everybody's been making a joke out of this. Maybe you should be getting counselling."

"I do all right with the boys sometimes," Zanske said. "I get along with the Gates boys from Braddock, but they just got evicted and I can't find them."

"They don't pack knives, those two?"

"Listen," Zanske said. "Lucia Ramos's psychologist thinks she knifed me because she was having some kind of panic reaction to the way I look. That's what she's getting out of these cozy little chats they're having. Whenever I bump into Lucia at school now, she runs away screaming. Last night I saw Mary Juventus at Airport Beach and she basically did the same thing. I mean, maybe it's *counterproductive* to follow up on the girls."

"I'll tell Guidance to lay off," Dankilow said. "It doesn't make that much difference. We'll try again next year."

At times like this, Zanske realized that he and Dankilow shared an unspoken, slightly shameful understanding of Zanske's job: that it was largely hollow labor; that he was largely a warm body, not the worst by far in the Education Department; that the vast majority of chronic truants dropped out, left town, or simply disappeared, and would do so whether Zanske kept after them or not.

"Rascati got his paws on Mary, you know," he said.

"Yeah?"

"You were asking about him, right? Well, he had a pretty lively day—or I don't know about the day, but last night he and Mary had a conference at which they discussed and then acted on certain sexual matters."

"Yeah?"

"Then he left her in the car and went down to the far end of Airport Beach and tried to fence some jewelry, and three guys robbed him and slit his nose open, like in *Chinatown*."

"Jesus," Dankilow said.

Zanske reported that he had taken Rascati to the hospital and that a friend of his had driven Mary home. Mary had been left to explain to her parents why their car was stranded at the airport.

"I must be losing my grip," Zanske said. "I was sitting there lecturing the kid about the words to 'America the Beautiful,' and his nose was half cut off."

It was hot again today. After hanging up, Zanske lay for a while on his back, in front of the fan. Then he dressed and went shopping. He returned and lay shirtless on the carpet again, with a sofa cushion for a pillow, and watched the Red Sox on Channel 38. The sound of the fan was like the sound of an airplane droning. In the middle innings, when the team was losing by eleven runs, he drove off to Dairy Queen for a milk shake. When he came back, the phone was ringing. "You should see my face," Rascati told him when he answered. "I'm gonna be ugly as you." Rascati's voice sounded stuffy.

Zanske, who had expected Scottnicki, asked angrily, "Where'd you get this number, anyway?"

"I looked in the phone book under 'ugly.' "

"You were as ugly as me *before* that guy sliced you."

"Did that hurt, when that girl got you?"

"You know where she did it."

"It didn't hurt?"

Zanske winced, remembering. There had been a ripping feeling—very frightening, but little pain.

"She was cutting your padding, man. She was trying to get through your padding, but she didn't make it. My face felt half ripped off. I never felt anything like that in my life. Those guys could've killed me, but I guess they weren't going to do that for a couple of necklaces. After you left, the cops wanted to talk in the emergency room, and I said no way. They'd definitely kill me if they heard I talked to the cops. I got all this cotton and shit stuffed up my nose."

"You going to come over and clean out my car?" Zanske asked. "Is that why you called? You messed up my Friday night, now you're messing up my holiday weekend."

"Right," Rascati said. "Your holiday weekend. What're your big plans?"

"Shut up."

"Washing your armpits?"

"I said shut up."

"You must have to use a mop. We should go over to Airport Beach. Drink a few beers. Be stabbed brothers together."

"Christ," Zanske said. "I can see *that* getting around."

"C'mon," Rascati said irritably. "Don't be no little person."

"I am not a little person!" Zanske roared. It came out like an explosion. It left him breathless. His ribs seemed to be vibrating. After an instant, he realized that Rascati, having trapped him, was laughing. Rascati laughed for quite a while. "You're telling me," he said, and hung up.

When younger, Zanske sometimes had imagined a pretty girl telling him he was a decent guy, and perhaps giving him a neck rub. The ends of her hair tingled his shoulders. Perhaps she had her shirt off for some reason (this always happened because of some unrelated event, a kind of celestial good fortune or a God-inspired combination of circumstances) and she said it was all right, she didn't mind him seeing. Now Zanske reverted to this pipe dream for the first time in years. He proceeded to have a bad afternoon. It seemed to him, as it sometimes used to, that his life was like the trip he had taken years ago to Hammonasset on Senior Skip Day—that he was the sort of person who went to the beach and only got as far as the parking lot. Most of the students at the high school were sexually active, but Zanske never had been. It irked him now that Rascati, at a third his age, was doing things he didn't even let himself imagine. Zanske had never aspired to be a member of the National Honor Society. Rascati was the kind of kid Zanske had admired when he was in high school. He would have been so successfully evil himself. Once again, he realized, he was being left behind.

That night a thunderstorm—the first of the year—washed over Airport Beach. People dashed for their cars through hissing curtains of water that turned the ground to thin gray mud. Everyone drove off except for Zanske and Scottnicki, who never budged.

Twenty minutes later, a huge plane roared overhead. (Zanske read in the paper the next day that it was a Boeing 737 that had had a problem with one of its engines and had been diverted from Bradley because the storm was more severe there.) It floated past like a spaceship or a prehistoric bird, then banged on the runway, dwindled in size, and stopped. In the distance, a train of emergency vehicles appeared, toylike, wailing and beeping. The twinkling lights curved along the road, made a line between the hangars, trailed out onto the runway, and encircled the plane, which had its own flashing lights at the ends of the wings and atop the tail. After a few minutes the sirens halted, and there was no sound but the dripping of water and the distant whining of engines. The clouds were low and ragged, and the colored lights moved against the wet skin of the plane.

Zanske stood with the car door open, his feet in the sand, watching. He was shivering. He glanced around and saw Scottnicki's pickup to the left, and, to the right, much farther off, one other car. They weren't the only ones here after all, he thought with a pang of disappointment, unless the car belonged to Mary Juventus's parents and they hadn't collected it yet. Rascati hadn't seen this, he told himself; Rascati hadn't been here. Zanske had the sense that he was being rewarded with a privileged glimpse of something after years of persistent effort.

Eventually he got back in the car. "That never happened since I've been coming here," he told Scottnicki. "That never happened in twenty-five years."

Scottnicki was silent, holding his beer can between his legs, staring straight ahead. It turned out this wasn't from a sense of wonder. He came to after a minute, and looked at Zanske as if Zanske had gone crazy. "So what?" he asked.

TEENA

THE BLESSED SAINTS CHURCH Summer Work/Study
Program ran Mondays through Fridays, from
eight-thirty to five. Reluctantly, Ricardo Maldonado,
who taught honors math to freshmen and sophomores
at the high school, got Teena Malvez involved. There
was a "scholarship"—a "slave wage," as Maldonado
termed it—of twenty-five dollars a week. He had lived
at the Kennedy public-housing project as a teenager, a
block from where Teena now lived.

The work-study program was only for girls. After
mass each morning, they did clerical tasks in the administration building, stuffing and addressing envelopes for
the diocese and otherwise picking up the slack for the
women who were on vacation. They also helped prepare, serve, and clean up after free lunches for the elderly in the basement. They had their own lunches at
one-thirty and then attended group meetings—during
which they had English instruction or gave book re-
ports—from two to three. For the next two hours, they

115

read in the library, which had no fashion magazines, or held one-on-ones—private talks—with Mrs. Gale, the program director, or played volleyball. A net was strung in a corner of the parking lot by the fence that enclosed the church, the rectory, the elementary school, and the administration offices. The buildings were of grim, soot-darkened brick, and the girls understood that the fence, which had sharply pointed metal stakes nine or ten feet high, was intended to keep the boys out.

As the summer passed, Teena nevertheless found a boyfriend. He was much older than she was. On a Wednesday in August, Ricardo Maldonado met his wife and Teena at Pizza Hut after Cathy Maldonado had driven Teena to and from a women's center in New Haven. Teena had seen a presentation on birth control. She had been given a package of condoms and had been fitted with a diaphragm in case there were problems in persuading her partner to use the condoms. Cathy had posed as Teena's mother.

The two women ate glumly, while Maldonado fished around for things to talk about. That was a mistake, because he discovered that Teena was "working" this weekend; the eleven girls in the summer program, all Hispanic, aged thirteen to sixteen, would be on duty Saturday and Sunday, from noon until ten, as the clean-up crew for the Blessed Saints summer fair. The fair featured polka bands in the afternoon and a group playing "easy-listening classics" Saturday night. The girls would wipe off tables, pick up litter, and empty the garbage from the backs of the food tents. They were supposed to wear white blouses and black skirts.

"They'd never have white girls doing that at the Hispanic festival," Maldonado told Cathy. "They think that's work-study? They're turning them into scullery maids!" He had a few choice things to say about Father Sorber, who handled the church's social-service projects.

Maldonado's feelings about the work-study program had been mixed for some time. "It's their cloistered-Madonna class," he had told Teena during the second-to-last week of school. "A lot of girls hate it, but I think you need to be cloistered." Now he pointed out to Cathy and Teena that the program hadn't even succeeded at that.

Blessed Saints was a short walk from the Kennedy public-housing project, and at least one mass each day was celebrated in Spanish. Not many people from the Kennedy neighborhood went to the summer fair, which was understood to be an English-speaking event. There wasn't a lot of mixing between the two congregations. The Hispanic festival was held in September.

"Will you two cheer up?" Maldonado said.

"Keep your voice down," Cathy told him.

As Maldonado was paying for their sausage-and-onion pizza, Bobby Figuera and Tony Phillips came into the restaurant. Teena was surprised to see them: this Pizza Hut was a long way from the downtown. She looked out the window and saw Tony's car in the parking lot. Beyond that, trees loomed above the roof of a real-estate office. The two boys sat in the smoking section, and when they saw Maldonado they yelled across the room.

"How you doin', Mr. Maldonado?"

"What *you* doing there, Teena?"

"This somethin' we don't know about?"

"Shut up, stupid. His wife's sitting next to him."

"Hey! Mr. Maldonado! Hey! Mrs. Lukowski won't be giving *us* no more homework!"

Both boys had dropped out in the spring. Last fall, Bobby had grappled with Teena in the hallway of the high school, forcing a kiss on her while three of his friends watched. When she had gotten her mouth free, she had screamed, and Tom Massey had come out of his classroom to see what was going on. Bobby had let her go.

In the restaurant's parking lot, Cathy and Teena hugged. "Those birth-control people thought you were my mother!" Teena said.

Cathy was blonde and had light skin. "Let's just say they weren't asking a lot of questions," she told the girl. "Try to stay away from the parties, O.K.?" As she gave this warning, the skin around her eyes crinkled. Teena had noticed that Cathy often expressed affection by squinting.

Teena had been one of two freshman girls to make the junior-varsity cheerleading squad and she had become fast friends with the other, Sharon Zezeck. Sharon lived on Ivy Vine Lane. Teena had been out there several times to dinner, and once, thumbing through the Zezecks' atlas while the family discussed vacation plans, she had discovered that Puerto Rico wasn't represented under the "United States" section. The only place it appeared was as a small blob in a corner of a map of the

West Indies. When Teena pointed this out, Mr. Zezeck
sat down at his computer and wrote an angry letter to
Rand McNally.

Sharon and her family were on vacation now; they
were at the North Carolina beaches. Next week they
would go on to Disney World. Lately, out of jealousy,
Teena and her other close friend, Luz Pabon, had been
referring to the Kennedy public-housing project as "The
Magic Kingdom."

A few days before leaving, Sharon had told Teena,
"I can't believe this is happening. Jimmy and me used
to tell our parents we were the only kids in the world
who never went to Disney World." The two girls were
at Friendly's Restaurant, in the mall.

"I'm really happy for you," Teena said.

"I don't even know what I'm going to do there."

"You can do a lot in seven days."

"I wish you could come."

"I wish I could, too."

Sharon looked at Teena over her milk shake. After
a minute she said, "You're so pretty."

"What are you talking about?"

Sharon pushed the milk shake to one side and
leaned over the table. The two girls gripped each other's
forearms. Their faces were close. They were giggling.
"I'm afraid we'll be like strangers when I get back,"
Sharon said. "I'm afraid I'll be a different person when
this is over."

Luz Pabon, Teena's other friend, couldn't leave her
family's apartment on the sixth floor of Building A of
the Kennedy project for the entire month of August—

except on Sundays, for church. Her father, the pastor of Iglesia Pentecostal de Maria, was punishing her for having gone to Dominic Pappalardi's party. Luz hadn't gotten back from Dominic's condominium in Middletown until four in the morning. She wasn't supposed to go to parties at all. Neither was Teena. Both girls had been cautioned against parties almost from infancy.

Usually Luz was in bed by ten. The night of Dominic's party, Rev. Pabon had had the police out looking for her by eleven. Teena felt guilty because Luz had gone mostly to keep Teena company, and because Luz had done nothing wrong, whereas Teena had done the worst thing in the world, according to the Blessed Saints Summer Work/Study Program.

Luz's imprisonment was hot and boring. The air was sticky; the weather felt like guilt or a scolding. By the second week, she was sick of reading and disgusted with the television. Stratovision Cable refused to hook up to the housing project. Without it, reception was limited to two channels. Gino's wouldn't deliver pizza there, either, although Luz had saved some money and could afford to send out for it. The third time she called, the manager came on the phone and apologized; he said that pizza-delivery men had been robbed of their wallets at Kennedy, their pizzas had been taken, and their red-white-and-blue delivery cars had been hit with rocks and bottles. He said that if Luz came to pick up her pizza he would give her a free Pepsi.

Teena often visited Luz. On afternoons when Rev. Pabon wasn't around, Luz would tell Teena she wanted to be thinner. "I should diet, but when you're cooped up like this you're so bored you can't stop thinking about food," she said. She was upset because none of the men at the party had liked her.

Cale Street, where Teena lived, and Dorr and Levy and Draper streets were part of a neighborhood centered at the Kennedy project and somewhat isolated from the rest of the city by rubble and vacant lots. Factories had come down and nothing had gone up to replace them. The region around the railroad line was overgrown with weeds and studded with gutted cars and old tires. A wooden sign facing the Kennedy project had once announced "PRIME INDUSTRIAL LAND" and now read "ZAZZ!" and "LOLA." Two months ago, Teena had seen her own name up there, next to a heart. She didn't know who was responsible—it could have been any of six or seven boys. The next day it was painted over with another girl's name.

Cale Street had dilapidated two-family and three-family houses, whose apartments were mostly rented out under the Section 8 program. The road ran parallel to the Kennedy project, with an abandoned shopping center in between. Beyond the brick towers of the Kennedy apartments, traffic ripped along the I-91/I-84 connector, which came through the downtown on a huge earthen bank whose sides were covered with grass, litter, and forsythia bushes. Between the towers and the highway were a small park and a community swimming pool. The pool had been closed since mid-July, when broken glass had been found in the water for the third time in two weeks. City officials had refused to pay to have the pool cleaned out again.

In summer, there was a lot of sky and sun; bricks and piles of old cement baked in the heat; trees of heaven grew along the railroad tracks. When Luz looked out the window from the sixth floor, the rising slope of the city to the east—a thick pelt of buildings and tree-tops—was smeared with haze. At night, crickets chirped, and atop the hill a huge pocket of light glowed. That was the mall, which Luz could no longer visit. She often followed the strobes of the police cars and fire engines as they streaked off on their various emergencies. The factories and the stores had fled the downtown, but the civic machinery was still there. Sometimes, when it was very late, she would phone Teena and whisper, "There's cops all over your street!" It was plausible enough, so Teena got up to look; she slept on the couch and it wasn't far to the door. Once, standing on the porch at three in the morning, she surprised a raccoon halfway into the garbage can that belonged to the people upstairs. "It was great!" she told Luz. "He was so cute!"

"You're not supposed to see raccoons," Luz said grumpily. "You're supposed to get out of bed for nothing. You're supposed to get *mad*."

At that point, Teena wondered if Luz was going to ask about Dominic—she often did when she was grouchy. "Is Dominic there?" she would ask. "I suppose you don't want to talk to me? I suppose I'm *interrupting* something?"

Dominic Pappalardi probably was capable of saying whatever he needed to say to get whatever he wanted from fourteen-year-old girls. But Luz told Teena that most of the things Dominic had said about that night were true: Teena had been the prettiest girl at the party, and so on.

When Teena confided in Ricardo Maldonado, the teacher, he said, "This happens all the time, and I'm sick of it. You girls reach fourteen and you look like angels. The rich girls have zits. They're still flat half the time. They don't look so great. They get a chance to grow up. Meanwhile you guys get ambushed by boys who are ten years too old for you."

Several late-night phone calls later, Mr. Maldonado suggested that Teena should think about taking a trip to New Haven with Cathy. "We might have to give the church antipreggers program a boost," he said to Teena. She ended up going with Cathy to the birth-control clinic.

Dominic was twenty-six, roughly Mr. Maldonado's age. Teena mentioned that fact, weeks after the party and the trip to New Haven, on her porch, in the dark, when she finally got up the nerve to tell Dominic he couldn't come in. By then, she was terrified that she was pregnant. "You're as old as my algebra teacher!" she shrieked. "He would have stopped!"

"Quiet!" Dominic hissed. "O.K.!"

On that occasion, at least, it was easy to tell Dominic what to do. He had grown up on Cale Street; his parents lived there; he couldn't afford to be seen at midnight with a girl almost young enough to be his daughter. His parents didn't rent their house but owned it. Mr. Pappalardi was known to regret that he hadn't sold it twenty years ago, when the Kennedy project went up and the neighborhood population changed from Italian to black and Hispanic. Dominic had gone to UConn. and now worked for the state Transportation Department. While visiting Teena, he always parked his Mitsubishi Montero four blocks away and sneaked over. He obviously felt guilty about what had happened. When they had gone upstairs the first time, in his condominium, Dominic had mumbled several times, "I shouldn't be doing this." That night on the porch, when Teena started yelling, he simply left.

The Rev. Pabon claimed that the purpose of parties, at least in the neighborhood of the Kennedy project, was to pretend that winter didn't exist, and he said that anyone who pretended that winter didn't exist was a fool. Before locking Luz up for the rest of the summer, he marched her down to Cotlin Street, several blocks beyond the abandoned shopping center, and pointed through the chain-link fence at the orange snowplows lined up in rows outside the city garage. Luz said that she got his point and could they please go home. The temperature was almost ninety. People would think they were crazy. Rev. Pabon pressed her against the fence. "You think things are easy?" he yelled. "You think the world's a nice place?"

Dominic Pappalardi was tall. His face had sharp, pleasing angles. He danced well. Teena and Luz had run into him at the mall as he was coming out of the package store with supplies for his party. Although cynical by reflex to almost anything men or boys said, and warned against parties, Teena and Luz nonetheless thought this one—at Dominic's condominium, by the

Connecticut River, with the salsa music and the blue lightbulbs that made you think of the sky over a southern ocean at night, and with pretty and sophisticated women from New York and Hartford there, many of them invited by Dominic's equally handsome roommate—might make it possible to pretend that winter didn't exist. Especially, Luz said, since it was the last day of July. Afterward, Luz perversely claimed that she was glad she had gone, that it had been worth it, although she hadn't had a good time. These days, if Rev. Pabon was around when the subject was discussed, Luz would say she planned to do it again.

Sharon Zezeck, who got to go to plenty of parties in her neighborhood because, like Teena, she was a cheerleader, regularly complained that the parties were boring because the boys involved didn't like to dress up and didn't like to dance, although they were interested in other things. Teena knew by now that with Sharon and Cathy Maldonado a certain amount of cultural translation, as Mr. Maldonado put it, was necessary. Teena didn't tell Sharon that it was hard to imagine anyone from the Kennedy project being shy about dancing. And she didn't explain that at the parties around the Kennedy project couples often went upstairs or downstairs or to rooms in the back when a certain point was reached—usually about the time the slow music was played. That was what happened at parties, and you either went to them or you didn't.

Teena didn't have to explain this to Ricardo Maldonado, who had grown up in the neighborhood. Cathy Maldonado might have understood, except that she kept saying as she drove Teena to and from New Haven, "You don't have to tell me anything; you have a right to some privacy." Shortly after meeting Cathy, Teena had wanted to hug her and spill out her problems. But Cathy was too short and Teena too tall for comfortable hugging, and when they finally did embrace, after dinner at Pizza Hut, it was a quick, awkward thing. Driving back from New Haven, Cathy had seemed to concentrate on the traffic and on changing lanes, and had talked in a businesslike way. "My husband can be sarcastic," she told Teena. "If he says anything obnoxious about the Catholic Church or teenaged girls, just ignore him."

What Teena recalled afterward wasn't the warmth of the hug from Cathy in the parking lot but the odd feeling of holding the diaphragm container. On the drive back from New Haven, she had kept fingering it through the white paper bag that carried the name and phone number of the women's center. The bag also held a box of ten condoms and a tube of Gynol, but the box was like any box and the tube felt solid and ordinary, like a tube of toothpaste. It was the diaphragm and its weirdly streamlined case that she couldn't get used to. The package and its contents were light, insubstantial, buff-colored, medical, and alien. Nothing else she owned felt or looked like that. Teena didn't tell Cathy—who grilled her, "You understand how to use it, right? You're going to use it if you need to, right? You're not going to forget, right?"—that she couldn't imagine actually using it. She also couldn't imagine asking Dominic to put on a condom.

"Lola! Baby! You have squashed my heart! You have dropped my heart in the dirt and you have stepped on it!"

That was Bobby Figuera; Teena was cutting across the parking lot of the boarded-up shopping center, which was where people from the Kennedy project worked on their cars. Bobby and his brother Angel had the hood up on Angel's Buick. Bobby waved his arms. "I am miserable!" he yelled. "I love you!" He followed Teena across the street, calling to her until Teena asked the housing project's foot-patrol officer to shut him up.

When she reached the Pabons' apartment, Luz said, "We're watching cars on the highway today. It's one of the exciting things we do here in the Magic Kingdom, to pass the time and everything. One car, this thing came out and filled up like a bag and floated all the way down onto DeWitt Street. I think it was some guy's shirt."

"I brought you a grapefruit," Teena said, reaching into her purse.

"I'd rather have some guy with his shirt off."

Rev. Pabon was gentle about Luz's punishment. He brought her books from the library two or three times a week, and she refused to open them. Luz had always gotten straight A's, and this sudden hatred of books worried him. Although he spoke Spanish at the church, Rev. Pabon allowed only English in the apartment, a rule the two girls were breaking at the moment. (Teena's mother had the same rule, but these days she spent most of her time in New Britain with her

127

boyfriend and was rarely there to enforce it.) This morning, Luz looked tense and unhappy. She hadn't combed or brushed her hair—it was around her head like a bush, and it partly covered her face. She wore an old T-shirt and gray sweatpants, and her lower lip stuck out, as it did when she was angry.

When Teena found out that Rev. Pabon wasn't in, she smiled and grabbed Luz's arm and whispered to her. Luz's face brightened. She pounded Teena on the back. Mrs. Pabon was in the kitchen and couldn't hear them, and Luz's three younger brothers, parked in front of the television, rarely showed any interest in anything Luz said to anyone. The girls hugged and squealed.

Teena wasn't pregnant. She had been unable to tell Cathy Maldonado how worried she was; Luz had been her only support. Cathy thought it had happened only twice, at Dominic's place, and that Dominic had phoned her a few times. Because of Cathy's affectionate disinterest in Teena's personal affairs, Teena hadn't been able to explain that Dominic had visited her four times since the party. He had discovered that she was usually alone on Cale Street.

"Good news!" Luz yelled. "Good news in the Magic Kingdom!" Then she whispered, "I'll call you later. I'm sneaking out. Those guys sleep like rocks."

For the church fair, workmen had erected a stage against the side of the Blessed Saints rectory. There was a wooden dance floor and there were booths serving ice cream, peach shortcake, kielbasa, hamburgers, and fried dough. The booths were clustered at the far end of the dance floor, and tents for eating and sitting ran up to the stage on each side. Separate areas had been set up for beer and bingo. The tents had yellow and white stripes and looked cheerful against the dark bricks of the church. A banner announcing the fair in red letters hung on the fence. When Teena arrived at quarter to twelve, the first of the polka bands was unpacking its instruments on the stage and Mrs. Gale was handing out large red buttons that said "BLESSED SAINTS CHURCH!"

Mrs. Gale rarely looked at Teena these days and almost never talked to her. Teena had confessed to Mrs. Gale during a one-on-one two days after Dominic's party and had upset Mrs. Gale a great deal.

"She should be counselling you," Maldonado said during one of Teena's late-night phone calls. "What's going on here?"

As Teena got her button from Mrs. Gale, she said, "I have a white blouse, but I don't have a black skirt. Are these pants all right?"

"They're better than bicycle shorts," Mrs. Gale said.

The second day of the work-study program, Father Sorber had taken Teena aside and explained that bicycle shorts shouldn't be worn around the church.

By four, the fair was very crowded. Teena and Sonia Velez had been assigned to one of the tents near the stage. They cleared plates and wiped tables. There were many parents here with young children, but Teena saw few teenagers, and she didn't recognize anyone from the high school. The music was cheerful and the dance floor was crowded, and Sonia kept making sarcastic comments about the dancing. "They dance like cows," she complained as she and Teena visited the trash barrels behind the kielbasa tent. "What is this shit?"

At five-thirty, Father Sorber gave a blessing, and the master of ceremonies introduced officials connected with the fair. Eventually he thanked the work-study girls for helping. Teena and the others were asked to stand on the dance floor and wave. They did, and everyone clapped, and Teena thought she heard several wolf whistles.

That night Bobby Figuera fell off the bridge that carried the interstate connector over DeWitt Street. Young men from the Kennedy project sometimes climbed over the chain-link fence that extended above the guardrail and then held on with one hand and jammed their toes into the upper of the two grooves that ran along the cement side of the bridge. From the Kennedy project, DeWitt Street went under the connecting highway and directly up the east-side hill to the mall. Whatever was painted there got noticed. Bobby fell thirty feet to the road.

Teena received the news in installments. "There's police cars all over DeWitt Street!" Luz whispered by phone at two-thirty in the morning. Teena replied that she was tired and didn't want to get up. Around three, someone tapped on the porch window.

Teena almost leaped off the couch.

"Dominic?" she said fearfully.

But it was Luz. She had sneaked out of her parents' apartment. She said the ambulance had left by the time she reached DeWitt Street, but several people had told her it was Bobby. "He was screaming," Luz said, "in the middle of the road."

"You'd better go back. Your father's going to catch you."

"I heard some people tried to help him up. That wasn't real smart. Do you have any eggs? I want to go over to Gino's Pizza and throw eggs at their windows."

"You can't do that!"

"No? Look, it's too bad it's so late. I wanted to go in there, get my free Pepsi that they give you 'cause they won't deliver three blocks down the street, and throw it at the guy. But they're closed."

"Go home, Luz," Teena said. "I'm sleepy. You're going to get in trouble."

"They go halfway to Middletown but they won't deliver to Kennedy."

"You better go home."

"My father wrecked my diet."

"How did he do that?"

"He bought a bag of Doritos and put it in my lap," Luz said.

Luz went home eventually. She called Teena again at seven-thirty in the morning. She said she had run into Tony Phillips in the Kennedy courtyard on her way back from Cale Street. That was around four in the morning. Tony had been at the hospital. He said Bobby Figuera had two broken legs. Luz added, "Bobby was putting your name on the bridge."

Teena filled the apartment with a shriek.

"I can see it from here," Luz said. "Out the

window. I just figured it out. I don't think anybody else did. Tony didn't say anything about it last night."

"Who will take it down?"

"Listen," Luz said. "Bobby's not real smart, O.K.? He spelled it wrong."

"I don't care!"

"He's got a heart up there, and a 'T' and an 'I.' There's part of an 'N' too. It looks like 'T-I-I.' There's a lot of other stuff already up there. It doesn't stick out."

Teena wanted to visit Luz, but it was Sunday and Luz had to spend the day at Iglesia Pentecostal de Maria. In fact, she had to hang up right now. "Poor Bobby," she said. "This could make you famous."

"Don't tell anyone!"

Felicia Malvez, Teena's mother, swung by the apartment at eleven. She had worked the night at Conway Gates Convalescent Home, where she was a nurse's aide. She took nursing courses during the day at C.C.S.U., in New Britain. That was where her boyfriend, Gabriel, lived. This was the first time Teena had seen her mother in three days. She told Felicia about Bobby Figuera and explained that she couldn't spend the day with Felicia at Gabriel's apartment because she was supposed to clean up at the church fair.

"You're working *weekends?*" Felicia yelled. "They paying you extra for this?" It was the same question Mr. Maldonado had asked.

"No," Teena said.

Shortly after that, Angel Figuera—Bobby's brother—showed up. Angel wanted to know if Teena was going to visit Bobby in the hospital.

Felicia met him at the porch door. "She didn't tell him to fall off no bridge," she said.

"Yeah, but she drove him crazy. She drove him crazy every time she came around Kennedy and she still came around Kennedy."

"Am I supposed to lock myself in my room?" Teena asked.

Felicia said she would call the police if Angel didn't leave. Angel said Teena should show respect for his brother. He said she and her mother would be sorry if she didn't. Then he left.

Felicia wanted Teena to forget the church fair and come to New Britain.

"But I don't like Gabriel," Teena told her.

"He's never done anything to you."

"I don't like the way he looks at me."

Felicia raised her hand, palm open. "I'll slap you!"

Dominic Pappalardi walked into the middle of the argument. He was halfway across the porch before he heard them, and by then Felicia had seen him. Teena wondered if he was drunk; he didn't look drunk, but she couldn't understand what would make him come here in broad daylight. Glared at by Felicia, Dominic smiled and glanced at the ceiling of the porch, as if he expected it to fall on him. "Well," he said coolly, "I guess *this* was a mistake. I'll be moving along now."

Felicia went right after him, and Teena heard her yelling around the corner. Her voice was shrill; Dominic's was deep and sounded calm. He and Felicia had grown up together on Cale Street.

When Felicia returned, she slapped Teena twice,

hard. In the ensuing argument, she asked if something also had happened between Teena and Bobby Figuera.

"No!" Teena howled.

"You're luckier than you deserve to be," Felicia said bitterly.

Teena was shocked to find out what her mother meant by that. She meant Dominic had been using condoms. "You asked him that?" Teena said, horrified.

It was true that Teena hadn't watched very closely during her dark encounters with Dominic. She had been embarrassed and nervous; she had spent most of her time staring at the ceiling.

"It's true. When you girls are pretty, you're prettier than anything. Prettier than the blondes, prettier than the Ivy Vine Lane girls. Everybody else gets time to grow up. They get to wait until they're sixteen or seventeen."

It was evening, and the Maldonados looked as if they had headaches. They were sitting at a table on the small patio that jutted into their backyard. Mr. Maldonado had his forehead in his palms. He was small and trim. For Cathy's sake, he spoke English. He looked up and took a sip of beer. Teena had a can of Pepsi, which she placed every once in a while against her forehead. The Maldonados had picked her up after the church fair. Teena had phoned from Cale Street, and Felicia—who always caved in before teachers, guidance counsellors, and principals—had caved in before Maldonado. Teena would stay here for a few days where Angel Figuera and Dominic couldn't find her. The Maldonados would drive her to and from the work-study program. Cathy said it was no trouble; she went down the interstate connector every morning on her way to work in New Haven.

"We get all these girls who are smart until they hit thirteen," Maldonado said. "Then they fall off a cliff. If you can just make it through the next few years, you're all right. Luz can do it. I'm not even worried about Luz. How old did you say this guy was? Twenty-eight?" No one answered him. "I wish you looked more like Luz," he said.

"Shut up," Cathy told him. "Teena looks like Natalie Wood in *West Side Story*. She could play Maria."

It was dark and the air was finally cooling. Cathy asked a few questions about how often Teena's mother was around. "She must have done a pretty good job with you, or you wouldn't be where you are," she said. "You get A's from Ricardo. That's not too bad, even if he's a pushover."

"You better goddam well keep getting A's," Ricardo said.

The Maldonados' house was on the west side of town. Two bedrooms were tucked upstairs, under the roof, and there was a rusty fence along one side of the yard. Beyond it a vacation trailer loomed whitely— the Maldonados' neighbors had parked it on the grass. It looked as though it had been there for ten years. Crickets throbbed and haze fell from the trees.

Teena asked, "Can they take my name off?"

" 'They'? Who's 'they'?"

"I don't know."

"I hope you don't mean *me*," Maldonado said. "I'm not going up there."

They ended up talking about the church festival. The Maldonados hadn't gone; it wasn't their sort of party, and in any case Ricardo said he couldn't have tolerated the sight of the Hispanic girls cleaning up the polka crowd's mess. He didn't seem to have much to do with the church, although he had gotten Teena into the work-study program.

Teena, steeping herself in the suburban quiet and the grays and blacks of the evening said, "A lot of them were fat. And none of them could dance."

"No kidding," Cathy said.

"There was nothing special about them."

The Maldonados looked at each other. "I take it all back," Maldonado told his wife. "If she's gotten that out of it, I'm going to call up Father Sorber and tell him his program's worth a million bucks."

Teena and Cathy listened to *West Side Story* in the living room for a while, chatting and looking at the pictures that came with the compact disk, before Cathy went to bed at ten-thirty. (Maldonado, excusing himself, told Teena in Spanish that he was sorry that Cathy seemed to think that Leonard Bernstein was the height of Puerto Rican culture.) After Cathy had said good night, Teena watched cable TV for an hour, sifting through the programs. If Stratovision Cable wasn't hooked up to the Kennedy project, it wasn't hooked up to Cale Street, either.

Around midnight, Teena quietly opened the back door and stood on the deck in the white nightgown she had brought from home in a paper bag. She remembered the relative quiet of the outlying neighborhoods from visiting Sharon. She wondered if Sharon really would be so changed by her vacation at Disney World that the two of them would feel like strangers when they saw each other again. Two weeks had passed. Out here, no music blared from open windows. No one was laughing or yelling in the street or roaring around in cars or on motorcycles; there were no sirens from police cruisers or fire engines. The houses on either side were dark; a single light shone from a window onto the backyard that adjoined the Maldonados' backyard, and beyond that, above a low roof, was a streetlamp.

In three days—bored, stranded far from the mall and from Luz's apartment—Teena would be eager to leave. But now what she longed to hear was that she could stay as long as she wanted to. On this night, she was a girl in a white nightgown on the west side of the city, feeling hopeful and softly singing to herself the words to "Maria."

Broken Violin

P EQUOT TRUST & SAFE DEPOSIT wanted to keep its name and to avoid an unfriendly corporate take-over, although the truth was it wasn't financially appealing enough to be taken over and it wasn't shaky enough to need a rescue. It was just a small local bank. But Home Dime, a somewhat larger local bank, liked the idea of buying somebody out, and so an amicable deal was in the works.

Men—there were no women involved other than Cheryl Donchuk—went to Kentucky Fried Chicken and talked strategy. They tried earnestly, it seemed, to feel important. It was doubtful that Cheryl Donchuk's technical advice was needed, but there had been enjoyment in the idea of hiring an analyst and swearing her to secrecy. These meetings were secret. Men wearing suits and carrying briefcases walked out of Home Dime at odd hours and crossed the street and sat in the chicken restaurant, and other men wearing suits and carrying briefcases drove over from Pequot Trust & Safe Deposit and got out of their cars in a group and came in and talked with them. Cheryl had been laid off from a New York investment bank and had accepted an offer of two months' consulting work—an offer relayed by her parents, who knew Home Dime's president. She was staying at her parents' house and visiting her Brooklyn apartment on weekends.

Home Dime might buy Pequot or it might not, and as far as Cheryl could tell, it wouldn't make any difference if it did or it didn't.

Thursday night, Wilbur Eldridge, holding a handrail, ratcheted up a grimy flight of stairs at South Central Connecticut State University. He had come to hear Ann Donchuk, Cheryl's mother, give a violin recital. Ann was a former student of his.

"Muddy Waters," said Cheryl. She was climbing ahead of him. Cheryl was thirty-one; Wilbur was eighty-nine.

He climbed slowly. "Muddy is the nickname?" he asked.

"No. On the record jackets it's not his nickname. It's his name. 'Mississippi' is the nickname. Muddy 'Mississippi' Waters. The others in the band are 'Pinetop,' 'Big Eyes,' and Luther 'Guitar, Jr.' Blues bands are big on nicknames."

"I see," Wilbur said.

Cheryl halted at the top and waited. "So I started thinking about how people in classical music don't have nicknames."

"No."

"Or we could call Mom 'The Smasher.' "

Monday, Ann Donchuk had dropped her violin on the floor, and it had more or less shattered. She would be playing Wilbur's at the recital.

They entered a small auditorium. There was a low stage in front. There were rising, semicircular rows of seats, and there were cinder-block walls painted gray. Thirty or forty students milled around. Wilbur sat in the front row, and Cheryl sat next to him.

Once the performance started, it seemed odd to Cheryl that no one had wondered whether it was safe to bring Wilbur to such an event. He was actually shaking. Ann hadn't given a recital in ten years, and this music—Prokofiev's Sonata No. 1 in F Minor for violin and piano, and Schubert's Piano Trio No. 2 in E-Flat Major—wasn't the sort anyone tackled casually. And Ann was performing on a strange violin. Wilbur had dug it out of his hall closet Monday night—he had been banned from playing at age eighty, some ten years after he had retired as chief of music instruction for the public school system. The violin hadn't been used for a long time, but it was the best available on short notice. Twice each day, meanwhile, Wilbur glued a nitroglycerin patch to his chest. He seemed to be in reasonable health otherwise, Cheryl told herself in an attempt at reassurance.

The accident with the violin had occurred while Ann was rehearsing in the dining room Monday afternoon. As she was turning a page with her left hand, the instrument squirted out from under her chin. Nothing like it had happened in some fifty years of playing. The

violin ricocheted off the edge of the dining room table,
and she snatched at it but missed. It landed facedown on
the floor a foot beyond the fringe of the rug. The bridge
broke off. The face split neatly—there was a crack an
eighth of an inch wide that ran almost perfectly through
the F holes. The neck separated from the body, and the
front plate popped up from the case on the left side.

Ann made three phone calls from reflex—to her
husband, Doug, at his office, to Wilbur Eldridge at his
house on Thorpe Street, and to Cheryl at the bank.
Cheryl sounded as if she'd been interrupted—she wasn't
very sympathetic. "They should have straps on them,
like binoculars," she said.

The violin was worth—or had been worth—over
thirty thousand dollars. Ann's father had bought it in
1943. They had gone into New York with Wilbur and
had inspected dozens. Ann was fifteen at the time. Her
father agreed to pay eighteen-hundred and left a three-
hundred-dollar deposit. He was a buffer at International
Silver, and it took him a while to find a bank that would
loan him the balance. He was ten years paying off the
loan. Later he told Ann that he wanted to own something that had survived since 1730 at a time when the
family was living from day to day, fearing bad news.
Back then, Ann's older brother was serving on a de-
stroyer in the Pacific.

Ann's father had died ten years ago, and Wilbur Eldridge was now very old. After phoning Wilbur and
telling him she might need his violin, Ann paused for a
few minutes and then made a fourth call. She thought of
information travelling in lines, past flowering dogwood

trees, the supermarket, and an old silver factory that was being converted into condominiums. Thinking about paths of information was better than thinking about the violin.

The love of classical music grew here and there in Connecticut, like a weed. A certain "music nerd," as Cheryl referred to Ann's friends, had to be told what had happened. George Sarofis's number was stuck to the door of the refrigerator by a green plastic magnet. He lived in Waterbury and was the best hope for a good repair.

At dinner, Ann admitted glumly that she hadn't adjusted the insurance in ten or fifteen years—the instrument was covered for only twenty thousand dollars. That night she drove to Waterbury and delivered it to Sarofis.

"Sarofis can fix it," Wilbur Eldridge said. It was early Thursday evening, and Cheryl was driving him to the recital. "But it's going to take a while. He can't hurry around down there in his basement, with his clamps and his pots of glue."

Cheryl imagined someone who looked like a troll. Sarofis probably did, given the way some of her mother's other music friends looked. "I'm surprised he can fix it at all," she said.

"It's hard to tell how it will sound," Wilbur admitted.

They worked their way through successive barricades of stoplights on the way to the interstate, and Cheryl wondered at the ease of their conversation. It had taken her a long time to escape the combination of guilt and authority that Wilbur represented, although none of it was his fault. Wilbur had studied in New York in 1919 and 1920 with a famous violin teacher, and Cheryl had studied briefly with Wilbur when she was in grade school. Her attitude had now come round to the extent that occasionally she would mention at parties that she had taken violin lessons from someone who had taken violin lessons from someone who had once played string quartets with Brahms. Even now she felt guilt over her acid, little-girl sulks of twenty years ago and over her embarrassing laziness. She hadn't practiced. "I don't see why anybody would want to do something this stupid," she had once told Wilbur in the cool, mahogany-darkened sanctuary of his living room.

Back then, Wilbur had regularly played the Brahms and Mendelssohn concertos with the Hartford and New Haven symphonies, and the show-off Paganini pieces; he had performed every two years or so with the local orchestra. That was in addition to running the school music curriculum at a time when there were several youth symphonies. He also went to Yale periodically for chamber-music performances. Cheryl knew this because of the steady connection between Wilbur and her mother. Ann had been his first private pupil. Two evenings a week Ann had gone to Wilbur's house. They both seemed to enjoy these sessions; Wilbur was a busy man, and perhaps it was a form of relaxation for him. Ann's father paid more for the lessons than Wilbur charged, because he had found out that Wilbur's rate was unreasonably low, and Wilbur put the money, all of it, into an account to be used when Ann went to college. Ann could get tears in her eyes talking about this. She seemed to feel that America, and the city, had worked back then, and she implied that the city had been full of cooperative, neighborly people who did touching and generous things for one another.

It had been hard for Ann to recover from the deep pleasure she'd felt as a child—the pleasure of making her father proud and of learning to do something difficult and of discovering the remarkable intelligence and beauty hidden in music written two or three hundred years ago. The result was that she tried to repeat the process with her children. Aside from the scandal of Cheryl's lessons with Wilbur, there were the occasions—increasingly rare—when Ann suggested family trios. "I'd rather jump off a cliff," Cheryl's brother, Brian, would say. "I'd rather pound nails through my toes," Cheryl would say. "I'd rather use my violin for a canoe paddle."

Trios were theoretically possible, because Brian had been switched from violin to piano after Ann and Doug found out he was getting off the school bus four stops early every day—more than a mile from home. It turned out that the violin he toted to and from the school symphony had made him such a tasty target that some of the other kids on the bus cheerfully and routinely beat him up if he got off at his usual stop.

It was a slightly rougher neighborhood than they were used to. Cheryl and Brian knew whom to blame for this change; it had occurred when Cheryl was seven and Brian was five, and it was the fault of Wilbur and

145

of the various doctors in town. They were addicted to string quartets. As a result, there were always doctors showing up to play quartets with Ann—some of them associates of Wilbur, whose brother was a surgeon, and some of them friends of Ann's from the orchestra. They arrived at night after hospital rounds and supper and made excruciating sounds until midnight. When someone was late, which was often, Doug, who called himself the world's worst violist, would fill in. If the missing physician was a cellist, Doug would be told to play the same music an octave or two octaves higher. Doug Donchuk was a science teacher until the doctors talked him into going to medical school at the age of thirty-three.

The family's suburban, split-level house was sold to free up some money, and the two kids were transported away from their friends to the second floor of a two-family house on Loudner Street. Bedrooms that were new and had relatively clean paint were traded for bedrooms that shed olive-colored flakes and had wheezing steam radiators. Cheryl and Brian were furious, but Ann and Doug had never been happier. The move didn't bother them—they were transforming their lives.

On the nights when there weren't string quartets, there was Ann's practicing—the endless, agonizing, scratchy phrases repeated over and over, knifing through the walls with remarkable ease. Years later, when Cheryl first heard about the neutron bomb, she called Ann from New York. "That's what it was like!" she yelled. "It was like the neutron bomb every night, right there in our apartment!"

Accompanying Ann on the piano was Juan Brac-
queia, a small man in his early sixties, a bachelor insurance agent who was perhaps the city's only Cuban
refugee. The Prokofiev Sonata No. 1 was slippery and
amelodic. Watching them play it made Cheryl think of
two fragile, elderly people piloting ten-speed bicycles
over a moonscape glazed with ice. The performance was
before a convention of music students from the state's
regional universities. An acquaintance who was on the
South Central State faculty had called Ann in late February and admitted she was under pressure to come up
with a program. Classical music didn't interest the faculty or the students, she said—the focus was on jazz,
rock, and marching band. The curriculum was intended
to produce high-school teachers, and there were not
many high-school orchestras or string programs anymore. It was unlikely the audience at such a performance would be large, Ann was told, but there was
supposed to be a classical recital at the convention nevertheless, and the faculty was having trouble finding
anyone to do it for a fifty-dollar honorarium.

Ann played first violin in the local symphony and
sometimes filled in in Danbury and Waterbury. She no
longer served as concertmaster anywhere. She had been
preparing diligently for the recital for two and a half
months—a performance like this wasn't something she
rattled off. At Yale (Cheryl thought), if the School of
Music staged a special event, it imported Isaac Stern.
Here, two people were plucked out of near retirement
from a rubbled mill town forty miles away.

Glancing sideways, Cheryl realized that Wilbur—still trembling noticeably—knew better than anybody else what kind of small and finicky adjustments were required to negotiate this music on a borrowed instrument. The chin rest had been altered and there were new strings, but that was the least of it. The performance seemed something to be gotten through rather than enjoyed; the point seemed to be merely to finish without disaster. Cheryl wondered whether her mother also was worried about dropping the violin. A lot of major errors would probably go unnoticed by this indifferent crowd, but a dropped violin wasn't one of them. Cheryl didn't see how her mother could stand upright under such pressure.

Ann looked pretty good. She wore a navy dress, pleated at the bottom, and high-heeled shoes. She was rather tall and stood erect. Her hair was gray. She did not give the impression that the fierce, icy demeanor she was displaying now was new for her—just not often assumed. Cheryl decided it had to do with standing up, with the increased vulnerability her mother must feel from being so exposed, and from the lack, in a duet, of a disguising crowd of other instruments. There was a picture of Ann at home that had been taken when she was giving a recital in college; her hair was still long then. Even so, in the picture she looked much like this: an exaggerated, ramrod-straight posture, a regal frown of concentration. Cheryl realized that aside from minor pieces at a few family weddings, she had never seen her mother perform standing up. Ann had done two or three concertos before Cheryl was born, and a handful of recitals. But most of her playing had been in the first seat of the local symphony.

As if zeroing in on the most crucial detail, Cheryl finally became aware of the glances the two musicians were throwing. In these looks, their age and vulnerability came out most clearly. It was apparent that it had taken decades to learn how to glance like that. Nothing was hidden—exhaustion, tension, the strain of keeping a tight cap on their nerves—because the level of concentration was so high; these things were bared because there was no energy left to disguise them. So honestly exposed, their faces were dignified in the way a bullfighter's face might be during a close maneuver with the cape. They concentrated only on giving and receiving specific, useful, immediate information on volume and timing. There were occasions when their eyes met, and there were occasions when one musician looked at the other, who was not looking, who was leading.

At the conclusion of the allegro, Wilbur exhaled noticeably. The side door opened, and Doug Donchuk walked down the front row, hunching to keep a low profile, and sat beside Cheryl. Others had snuck in earlier—the doctors were chronically late. There were five or six of the old group here, and none had been on time. It was an odd crowd. There were the physicians, a few other family friends, and three or four of Ann's music-nerd associates—frumpy, gentle, middle-aged men who filled the front rows of the symphony or sold tickets or ran the annual fund drives and who now sat listening with eyes closed and blissful looks on their faces. And scattered about the back rows were forty or fifty college students. There were no children, and there seemed to be no one else Cheryl's age.

Ann began the fourth movement and quickly stopped. She said, "I'm sorry" to Juan and paused to tune. Wilbur looked at Doug quizzically, and both winced. The music began again, firmly, and rasped to its conclusion. It seemed to Cheryl, who had turned in her seat, that some of the students were staring at the stage as if this difficult, atonal composition were being performed with dentists' drills.

When the first piece was finished, Cheryl automatically consulted the Xeroxed program in her lap and made a mental check-off. One item down and one to go. It was a childhood habit she hadn't indulged in years, a way of coping with experiences that were unpleasant and long. In this manner, she used to chart her way through the boredom of church services, and she had done the same thing through endless city symphony performances. When young, Cheryl and Brian would sit with their father somewhere in the middle of the high-school auditorium, surrounded by mink coats and wrinkled skin and a miasma of perfume, and Brian would whisper, "You and me and nine hundred old ladies." In recent years, much of the symphony's elderly audience had died off, and the symphony was dying with it. Performances were now given in a local theatre that had half the capacity of the school auditorium, because no new generation of listeners had arisen to replace these old women.

During intermission a professor took the stage and talked for a moment about the Schubert Trio in E-Flat

Major. It was similar to Beethoven's Fifth Symphony in that a theme from an earlier movement made a reappearance in the last, she said. Students from the various colleges should have studied Beethoven's Fifth in their classical-music appreciation courses, she pointed out. Several of the students left. When the professor had finished her talk, Ann and Juan reappeared with the cellist, and they began to play the Schubert trio.

The long, slow fuse lit in Cheryl's childhood had finally burned to the point where she enjoyed some classical music. For a long time she had hated it passionately and had blamed it for several years of unpopularity as a teenager. She angrily attributed to her parents the social buzz saw she had run into in junior high school, when she discovered that she was the only person who had never listened to the Rolling Stones or the Jefferson Airplane and the only person who had heard of Schubert and Handel. These days, at her New York apartment, she would listen occasionally to the more famous symphonies and to the Beethoven and Brahms piano concertos. There were passages that made her eyes fill, which she attributed not only to the beauty of the music but to the guilt accumulated during the years when her well-honed sarcasm was an effective, cutting weapon in the long, bittersweet war with her parents over what was beautiful and valuable, what was popular or embarrassing, what was worth extensive study and effort, what was considered fun. She still didn't listen to chamber music if she could avoid it; she hadn't gotten to that point yet. It lacked the breastbone-vibrating volume that the symphonies shared with rock, and she still associated it with the late-night string quartets that had tormented her sleep.

Accordingly, she was unprepared for the second movement of the Schubert trio—the astounding, simple melody that steps back and forth between major and minor keys and is based on an ancient Scandinavian folk melody about a sunset. Something she had expected to be nerve-racking was beautiful.

Ann's part wasn't nearly so critical, and she was sitting down, which meant that her lap was interposed between the violin and the floor. If this piece wasn't necessarily easier, it seemed that way, and by the second movement Cheryl realized that her mother was going to pull off this performance. In the fourth movement, Ann made a clear botch: a tangled phrase that she quit halfway through and picked up on the next measure. A few minutes later, another followed. Then the melody from the second movement reappeared, faster and more cheerful, and the piece was done.

The clapping quickly ended; the students rapidly exited; Wilbur and the various doctors ambled forward to the stage. Ann put the violin in its case. Cheryl sat for a minute to let her eyes clear. She didn't think anyone had noticed. The melody still rang in her ears.

They drove home in their various cars and met at the Taconic Crest Inn for dinner, which broke the spell—Cheryl had spent so much time next door at Kentucky Fried Chicken while the small-town bankers plotted their unnecessary merger that in the oppressive atmosphere her head cleared and her impatience returned. The Taconic Crest was a dark and venerable restaurant that she and Brian had called, as children, "the Chronic Death."

After dinner she drove Wilbur to his house on Thorpe Street. He, too, seemed irritable.

"I don't like it that the largest occupied building in this city is the hospital," he grumbled as they skirted its bulk. They went around the far side, past the neon signs marking the way to the emergency room, and stopped at the corner of Ballard to wait for the light.

"You were shaking like a leaf tonight," Cheryl told him.

"Yes," Wilbur said tiredly. "That usually happens when I watch your mother. When she performs like that, she's pushing her limit. She can handle more than you think she can, but I can never quite believe it in advance."

Cheryl looked out the windshield. She had half overheard a conversation yesterday between her parents to the effect that Wilbur's violin actually was slightly inferior to Ann's. Ann had explained that Wilbur hadn't needed as good an instrument. The matter of the limits of Ann's ability had come up long ago and had been accepted; she was not a professional in the sense that Wilbur had been a professional. To a greater extent than Wilbur, she had survived on practice and concentration.

"She has remarkable nerves," Wilbur said now. "They're a lot better than mine, thank God."

Cheryl wasn't used to attributing courage to her mother. For that matter, she often had to remind herself that her father was a physician, that he had made a career change when he was over thirty that few people would have had the guts to attempt. Neither of her parents was domineering or aggressive, and Cheryl tended to think of them as gentle, easygoing people living quietly in a backwater city. But in fact (she thought now) it was possible that she would never in her life do anything as frightening or difficult as her mother had done tonight or her father had done over twenty years ago.

"She didn't drop it," she said.

Wilbur looked at her sharply. "You can't be serious," he said.

Then, after a pause, he said, "For a minute there, I was afraid I was going to die."

The stoplight changed, but Cheryl, in shock, kept her foot on the brake. Wilbur looked at her in surprise. He was simply telling her something.

"That's what a performance is," he said. "It's been a while and I'd forgotten. It's like facing your own death, but of course in this case you have the chance to beat it off."

It was the question of chance and of beating things off that plagued Cheryl later. She lay in her parents' house, in the bed she had slept in as an adolescent. In the dark room, she squeezed her arms around her stomach, full of self-loathing.

She thought about a culture or a heritage that would allow people to shoulder an unusual load of skill and terror. It was one of life's secrets, apparently, passed from Wilbur to Ann and from Wilbur's medical friends to her father, and yet it had stopped without descending to her. She assumed that many people spent their lives without knowing it. One of its symptoms was an exchange of glances that had more business in them than any Cheryl had ever seen exchanged in the business world. No look Wilbur could share with her now could transfer this secret—it took years to learn, and the thought struck at her like the sight of a violin falling or of hell opening that she, unlike so many, had had the chance at it, and had refused to take it.

KING DAY

TWENTY-FIRST CENTURY GOLF was not supposed to open until eleven in the morning on Mondays, Wednesdays, and Fridays in January, because business was slow and because Lloyd Gomes, the winter manager, was taking a 9:00 A.M. accounting course at the University of Hartford. But on the morning of the third class, Gomes dropped the course, which was full of Malaysians pursuing business degrees under a program approved by the U.S. State Department, and came to work early.

It was snowing. There was snow in the parking lot, and George Gradki's old Cadillac Eldorado was there, too.

21st Century Golf had an "All-Weather Driving Centre"—a back room with a tee, a piece of artificial turf, a propane heater, and a garage door that opened electrically and faced the driving range. There were several flattened cigarette butts on the floor, and along the far edge the tiles had been ripped up and the joists ex-

157

exposed. Only the occasional snowflake reached Gradki, who was soon on the tee, trying out a sample set of graphite-shafted irons.

"I'm off that day," Gomes said into the telephone. He was sitting on a molded-plastic chair on the other side of the wall, behind the store counter. He could observe Gradki through a window. "You can't change your mind," he said. "We got this straight a month ago."

He was talking to James Paltamiento, who owned 21st Century Golf and three liquor stores. Paltamiento said he'd forgotten about Gomes's plans to go skiing on Martin Luther King Day, and he explained that he couldn't work in Gomes's stead because he was going to be at a regional bowling tournament in Massachusetts. The other person who could handle the shop, Enrique Colon, had been fired.

"Let me get this straight," Gomes said. "This is Martin Luther King Day, and you've got the day off, and I'm working." Gomes was black.

"I know it sounds bad," Paltamiento said. He explained that the tournament entry fee had been two hundred dollars and that three teammates were involved.

With his left hand, Gomes sifted through the golf tees displayed on the counter. There were perhaps five hundred of them in a container meant to resemble a giant golf ball. "Call Enrique," he said. Enrique, the former equipment manager, had been fired two months ago.

"No," Paltamiento said.

This stretch of the Franey Turnpike featured the

Yankee Maiden Motel, the now-defunct Nero's Drive-In theatre, Jack's Camper Service (external racks holding fibreglass shells for the backs of pickup trucks), and the Northeast Depot (truck trailers rusting in dead, two-foot-high weeds). Snow here resembled asbestos fallout. At the moment, it was coming down hard. An hour and a half ago, while walking to the university administration building to drop Bookkeeping III, Gomes had seen, on the far side of the parking lot, three Malaysian women floundering through the snow in long dresses and black veils. They were near a skeletal tree, and their figures were blurred and oddly sinister—all they seemed to be missing were scythes. Last fall Gomes had had a crush on a Malaysian student for several months—a girl he shared two classes with. She had told him she found snowstorms terrifying. They destroyed all the color in the landscape, and took away all the smells. The temperature in her home city on the South China Sea rarely dropped below eighty.

Gradki hit a lime-colored golf ball that made a modest arc and disappeared into the snow; there were perhaps three inches on the ground. The graphite-shafted irons he was using cost six hundred thirty-nine dollars. It was clear that Gradki wasn't going to buy them. Still, he was going to buy some irons at some point, because he was entitled to full credit for the Starburst clubs he'd gotten here last summer. The heads had been falling off, usually in midswing. It was a good thing no one had been hurt. The top of Gradki's nine iron had disappeared into a pond at Timberlin, for example, in Berlin, in September. After similar complaints from other golfers, Paltamiento had fired Colon, the equipment manager.

Starbursts were less expensive than other clubs. They were pushed enthusiastically by 21st Century Golf because the components were assembled in the basement and the profit margin was high. Colon wept; Paltamiento used a few words he shouldn't have; Colon called Paltamiento "white slime" and stormed out.

Gradki opened the door of the driving centre and asked for more balls. He was in his late sixties and retired. Gomes gave him a small bucket and listened as Gradki talked about Corey Pavin, the P.G.A. tour player. Gomes had discovered that some of the older men who came here developed crushes on professional golfers, in much the way thirteen-year-old girls developed infatuations with the models in fashion magazines. Gradki returned to the driving centre and hit two more balls, then came back and sat down, gasping. He suffered from emphysema.

"Pavin's gonna be the next Nicklaus," he said. Gradki could pass several hours this way. The accounting courses he kept dropping were boring, Gomes thought, but they were nothing compared to this.

There was a poster of Pavin on the wall above the golf shoes. He wore a shirt of bright orange and had a slim waist and a graceful swing. Gradki, by contrast, swung with an arthritic hunching of the shoulders followed by an axlike chop at the ball. Gomes was far from graceful himself. He had a stiff, upright stance and extended the index finger of his right hand down the shaft of whatever club he was using. Gomes was a par player and sometimes offered suggestions to customers, but he tried to avoid outright demonstrations. His parents were Cape Verdean. He had been born in Rhode Island and had moved to Connecticut when he was six. His mother and father were physical therapists, and theirs had been the only black family in a neighborhood of split-level houses washed by the sound of traffic on the interstate. As a kid, Gomes had been lonely and had skied by himself on winter afternoons at Mount Southington. In the summers, he had played a lot of golf. When he was sixteen, he had finished fifth in the state high-school golf tournament.

Enrique Colon used to help with the nightly chore of collecting the balls from the driving range. After the heavy rains in October, some of them had become embedded in the mud. Now the ground was frozen, and Gomes, working alone, had to pry them out with a crowbar.

When he was still in high school, Gomes used to walk to the turnpike from his subdivision, skirting a swamp and slogging in the dark over a ridge by a trap-rock quarry. (You had to know where you were going.) He would meet up with a Hispanic friend from school, Jesus Correia, who had come down the railroad tracks from one of the housing projects. Back then there was no store—only the driving range, owned by Palta-miento's predecessor, and a smaller building from which the buckets of golf balls were sold. Arriving well after the place had closed for the night, Gomes and Cor-reia would climb to the roof and watch the top half of the screen at the drive-in, which was visible beyond the fence marked with the 350 sign. "Baby!" Correia would yell whenever a naked actress ducked out of sight. *"Lola! No te vayas!"* The theatre had long since closed; the audience had disappeared. People watched their X-rated movies at home now, on videocassettes.

After Enrique Colon was fired, Gomes, who had been laid off in September from his full-time job at Oil-field Services & Supply Co., had taken on Colon's hours and had begun to work full-time. He didn't miss OSASCO, although he had worked there for seven years. For a long time, the firm had had the only build-ing on Industrial Terrace, which connected with the Fra-ney Turnpike a mile and a half south of the golf store. The lampposts marched prominently down the deserted boulevard, and cattails waved beyond the curbs. The place was largely swamp. Teenagers staged drag races there at night, and in the summer one occasionally saw snapping turtles squashed on the pavement. Gomes's job went with the fourth wave of layoffs, and it seemed to him that OSASCO had held onto him considerably longer than it might have. The supervisor in the Book-keeping Department explained that the company didn't want to lose all its younger employees. Gomes had been hired part-time during his junior year in college, when he was getting straight A's. He worked full-time over the summer, and the following fall was offered a raise if he would stay on. He began to take his accounting courses at night. Under that arrangement, he would have had his degree in two years if he hadn't kept drop-ping courses. He found the classrooms depressing at night; the professors appeared tired and uninterested, and the janitors went somnolently down the hallways with large rotary floor-polishers. After OSASCO tossed him out, he invested a thousand dollars in Mobil and Texaco stocks, out of pique, and these did well enough while he worked at the golf shop and passed his free time watching college basketball on the all-sports channel.

This morning marked the third time Gomes had fled Bookkeeping III—it seemed just as hard to face the stuff in the morning. Friday morning, he had loitered outside the room on the second floor, waiting for class to end so that his instructor could sign the form allowing him to withdraw. He found that his new ski gloves wouldn't fit in his coat pockets, and so he tucked them under his arm and reached for a Kleenex. The form was in his mouth and his head was down and the gloves were starting to slip as he wiped the fog from his glasses when the door opened and Haslinda Wahab came out. She regularly left class to smoke cigarettes in the hall.

"Zombie," she said to him.

"No!" Gomes exclaimed. "No!"

It was a word she often used in jest.

Haslinda was one of the few Malaysian women at the university who didn't wear a veil. She wore short skirts. The others wore long dresses and cooed and rustled quietly in the back of the room, like pigeons. They all studied very hard. Their tuitions were paid by the Malaysian government and in return these students would owe decades of work at government jobs.

The first day of school in the fall, before Gomes had quit Business Economics II, the admissions director had come into the room and asked for a volunteer to drive one of the Malaysian students to the Copaco meat plant in Bloomfield, where a butcher had agreed to slaughter chickens according to Muslim ritual. No one volunteered, so the director asked Gomes, who happened to be sitting nearby. The slaughterhouse wasn't far from the University of Hartford. Haslinda, who had been given orders from several of the other students, stared at the floor of Gomes's Honda. Her skin was as dark and smooth as the surface of a Coppertone bottle.

Before killing the first chicken, the butcher held it up for her to look at. "O.K.?" he said. Then, to the chicken, he said, "So long, snooks."

Gomes spoke with Haslinda occasionally after that. Her father was a forest ranger, distantly related to the king, and she was the fifth-ranked woman tennis player in Malaysia. Gomes's view of the world was not distorted by a haze of self-confidence, and the scene with the form in his mouth and the Kleenex over his eyes and Haslinda's contemptuous remark came up for replay, in sharp focus, nine or ten times over the course of the day at the golf shop. He grew still more depressed when the snow changed to rain. That often happened in Connecticut, but in recent years it also had been happening farther north, in Vermont. Gomes didn't want another threat to his skiing plans. Persuading Paltamiento to give him the day off was enough of a problem.

Shortly after five, he drove home through the drizzle. There were softened, Tupperware-like sheets of ice floating in the puddles. He entered his barn-shaped, redwood-stained apartment house and heard someone dribbling a basketball in the stairwell. Four young men were on the second-floor landing. Two sat on the steps. One leaned against the window and smoked a cigarette, and the fourth—the shortest—pumped the ball up and down on the carpeted cement. He kept his body motionless except for the arm and the hand. Sometimes this group broke into rap numbers, but apparently they weren't going to at the moment. Gomes was opening his door when Carol Jarvis flew from her apartment into the hallway, shrieking, "Leave! Leave!" She lived next door. The young men dropped fluidly down the stairs. After a minute the basketball resumed its cadence outside. On the wet sidewalk, it sounded like a whip cracking.

Carol and her husband, who were white, thought the young men who hung around the hallway were too interested in their adopted daughter, Chrissandra. Chrissandra, who had been born in Jamaica, was thirteen. Last week, Carol had asked Gomes for advice. She had blonde hair, graying, and glasses with wide lenses. As she leaned in the doorway, she trembled.

"They're not bad kids," he said.

"They never leave her alone."

Gomes didn't know what to tell her.

"They bother her at school," Carol said. "I guess she's supposed to be pregnant by the time she's fourteen. Maybe she should tone down the clothes, but she shouldn't *have* to tone down the clothes. She should be able to dress like the other girls."

Chrissandra had been at the top of the stairs a few

weeks ago, talking to these young men and arching her back over the railing, when Gomes came in from the parking lot. She had long hair and was wearing a jumpsuit. Gomes tripped on the stairs, and from above she regarded him coldly, the way, in his nightmares, Whitney Houston did.

That evening, Enrique Colon kept an eye on a cannister of chocolate ice cream that was rotating in the microwave oven in Gomes's apartment. Enrique was softening it up. Gomes had gotten Enrique to come over on his dinner break from his job at Kentucky Fried Chicken.

"Jim," Gomes told Paltamiento over the phone, "I took it seriously. I need the day off. What if I don't show up? Why don't you talk to him?"

Enrique Colon took the phone. He said to Paltamiento, "You ever cleaned out a French-fry vat?"

Colon was studying engineering. He had a short, punk-style haircut. He wore black pants and black high-top sneakers under his Kentucky Fried Chicken tunic. He played on his college golf team, and his swing was fluid and stylish—he had none of Gomes's awkwardness and idiosyncracies. As he listened on the phone, he lifted the ice cream out of the microwave and tested it with a fork.

Gomes took his bowl of ice cream, then putted a Pro Staff nervously across the living-room carpet. The ball was chased by his kitten. It was Gomes's opinion that Paltamiento hadn't trained Enrique sufficiently in assembling the Starburst clubs. That had been part of

the problem—not enough glue. But Gomes also sus-
pected that Paltamiento had decided that the golf shop's
customers weren't ready for an authority on golf who
happened to be Puerto Rican. They weren't a very en-
lightened crowd out there. They weren't the sort who
belonged to fancy country clubs, although the sort who
belonged to fancy country clubs probably wouldn't be
very welcoming, either.

And how were these customers ready for Gomes?
Gomes had a theory about that. He had decided, out on
the Franey Turnpike, that there was a belief in magic.
Golf was a difficult game, and playing it well had to do
with such logical matters as instruction and practice and
with how well coordinated you were. The golf shop's
customers didn't have much faith in these things. They
took a more mystical approach. People who came to
21st Century Golf tended to develop odd twitches and
to experiment with bizarre grips. And if the players on
the P.G.A. tour were regarded as gods, Gomes, for
some reason, was considered a minor oracle. He had
wire-rimmed glasses and thin shoulders; he looked stu-
dious and he had a mysterious accent. A number of the
customers seemed to think of him as someone who understood golf subverbally, essentially—the way Ned, in
Faulkner's *The Reivers,* understood horses. Gomes had
once heard the word "voodoo" waft in from the parking
lot. It might have been Gradki. Lately Gomes got a lot
of requests for lessons he wasn't qualified to teach, and
lately Gradki had begun to extend his right index finger
down the shaft of whatever club he was using.

Gomes took the phone from Enrique. "If I have to

work just because you're going bowling," he told Paltamiento, "I'll quit."

"I didn't have to hire you guys."

"Get Enrique to work. He wants the job."

"I thought you wanted the hours."

"It was his job."

"I'm going to have to think about this."

"There's some stuff I don't negotiate. I ski on Martin Luther King Day. That's it."

Sunday, in Vermont, it snowed relentlessly. Ba-
roque decoration was heaped in the trees. In the evening, Gomes sat on the living-room carpet of a ski
condominium and watched people coming and going
from a sauna down the hall. The condominium was
owned by his parents and two of their associates. Except
for an efficiency apartment in the basement, which was
always available to the owners and their families, the
place was usually rented. This weekend it was filled
with teachers from Massachusetts, who had escaped for
the Martin Luther King weekend. They had invited
Gomes up for a party. He had his back against the living-room wall. Down the hall the sauna door opened
and briefly he saw Cindy, a blonde who taught in a
school near Springfield and had insisted on skiing with
him most of the afternoon. It had been odd—had almost interfered with his sense of purpose. She wasn't
very good, and she made him nervous. Finally, she had
gotten tired and had gone down to the lodge. Gomes
always skied from the time the lifts opened until they
closed. He didn't even break for lunch.

Also in the sauna was Martie, a thin woman with dark hair whose eyes, without their glasses, looked puffed and white. She had a bandage on her forehead and had wrapped herself in a towel. The teachers had been here since Friday night. Gomes had spent Saturday at the golf shop and then had driven up Saturday evening. Enrique would work Monday—Paltamiento had relented.

Gomes kept to the edges of the party, but stayed up until two in the morning. Toward the end, he sat alone on the couch and speculated that if he ever got his accounting degree he could land a job, buy an all-terrain truck like a Jeep or an Isuzu Trooper—he liked them— and somehow save Haslinda. She wouldn't have to go back to Malaysia if she didn't want to. He knew it was a delusion to think she would necessarily want to be saved, and especially by him, but he had had a lot of beer. Occasionally he touched the spot on his left cheek—like a thawed place where someone had breathed against a frosted window—where Martie had kissed him before going to bed. She had come out of the sauna before the others, and they had started talking. Pulling her towel tightly around her, she had explained the bandage on her head: A student, still unidentified, had thrown a quarter from across the classroom and hit her above the left eye. She had fainted facedown on the edge of her desk, receiving a cut that required five stitches.

Gomes wasn't sure if her intent was romantic. It might have been solidarity. He knew that unlike his sister, an all-around success now in medical school, and unlike his parents, who had the reserved dignity of Bantu aristocrats, he belonged to another subgroup—a multiracial one consisting of awkward people who lived for brief moments when they didn't feel that way, for moments when they were confident and graceful. Such a moment had just come and gone, he worried—although most of the Martin Luther King weekend was such a time for him. That morning and afternoon, comfortably blubbered in his down coat, he had discovered that so much of his past had been spent skiing—he had invested so many adolescent winter afternoons at Mount Southington going up and down, up and down, all by himself—that the familiar self-absorption set in even when Cindy, the blonde, had decided to keep him company. He had hardly talked to her.

After he and Martie had visited for a while, he told her about Haslinda. He explained that he liked Haslinda and that nothing would come of it.

"Do you ever think about dating white women?" Martie asked—and the question, which came hesitantly, sent Gomes into a familiar, awkward, stiffening of his shoulders. It was something like his golf swing. Gomes said he didn't know how he felt about it. "It's complicated," he explained. He didn't add that his sister regularly told him she would never speak to him again if he did such a thing. She said she had too many friends—middle-class black women—who were lonely, who couldn't find anyone.

"It's complicated," he said again, and shortly after that Martie kissed him on the cheek and went off to bed.

At two-fifteen, Cindy, the blonde, swung the

Heidi-like shutters outward from the master bedroom, which, according to the ski-chalet architecture of this condo village, overlooked the living room and kitchen. She leaned out in her nightgown and dropped a beer can some fifteen feet into the kitchen wastebasket.

"You should sleep," she told Gomes. "Where's Martie?"

"Asleep."

Cindy regarded him with disappointment.

"Well, good night," she said.

"Good night."

He stayed up a while yet, and presently began to enjoy himself again. He knew he might have remained at home and attended King Day services, but he felt, once again, that he had accomplished something. Thousands of people went to Vermont and New Hampshire on the Martin Luther King weekend. The chances were high that they would pass the three days without even seeing someone who was black. Gomes was a good skier, and in a small way it mattered. He was not only good; skiing happened to be the one thing at which he was graceful. The sport wasn't like some foreign territory he had conquered but something deep, natural, and familiar. In Gomes's case it was unexpected; it surprised people; it was an indication that what a person could do well wasn't necessarily predictable. He was glad when Cindy had closed the shutters and he was by himself again, because he wanted to think about that. He didn't want to think about work and he didn't want to think about love, matters which were more complicated and, it seemed to him, less important.

Splat

OOK AT THE BLIMP," said Irene. She meant the
woman who ran the cash register at QuikMart.

Irene and her brother Andy were slouched in their
father Bill Stankowski's pickup truck, lethargic as cats,
and the clerk—huge and world-weary—was leaning
against the front of the convenience store. She was
wearing a yellow T-shirt and blue sweatpants, and she
was smoking a cigarette, and Stankowski felt sorry for
her. She seemed a symbol that the summer had col-
lapsed. It was a time of year when the air was thick with
haze and people grew tired of one another; when cars
overheated on the way home from Lake Winnipesaukee
and the world seemed to consist of highway medians
and parking lots stained with oil slicks and spilled milk-
shakes.

Stankowski's family hadn't even had a vacation.
What might have been a vacation had been passed in
moving from Indiana to Connecticut a month ago.
They had returned to their slightly rubbled ancestral

mill town after following Stankowski's wife, Beth, around the country as she pursued advanced degrees. Now she had a job in New Haven, and Stankowski, armed with a three-month certificate from a computer school—something no one seemed to care about—was driving a cement-mixing truck. Any vacation would have to wait until construction season ended in the winter. He turned into a parking space. Because Andy had had a rough morning and Stankowski didn't know what to say to him, he took the boy's hand and held it under his own on the shift knob.

"You know what that is?"

"Second."

"Great," said Irene. "I'm riding around in a pickup truck with a couple of fat guys holding hands."

"Jesus," Stankowski said.

"Shut up," Andy told her.

Irene was fifteen and wanted to go to the drugstore for makeup. She normally avoided the pickup, but Beth was off until midafternoon with the Omni, and Irene wanted the makeup now. Stankowski got out. In the QuikMart, it was cool and dark. He found the half-gallon milk jugs with the blue plastic tops, then waited with three other people for the clerk to finish her cigarette. There was mild condensation on the long freezer next to the checkout counter, and he touched it and thought of the comforting sweat that appeared on beer bottles when they sat in the back of the refrigerator in the summer. Then the clerk came in, and he paid and went out into the heat again and saw that Andy was the only one in the truck.

"So where is she?"

"She started talking to this guy. Over by Dunkin' Donuts."

"They went inside?"

"No. They got on his motorcycle."

"Seriously?"

"She's wearing shorts. She doesn't have a helmet or anything. If they hit something, she'll get splatted all over the road."

"Do you know this guy?"

"If they hit something, she'll get the skin ripped off her legs."

"Do you know this guy, Andy?"

"No."

"Are we supposed to wait for her?"

"She didn't say anything," Andy said. "She never says anything."

"What do you mean she never says anything? What are you talking about?"

"To me," Andy said.

Stankowski started the truck.

"If they hit something," Andy said, "she'll wish she was still fat."

Irene had been wearing a lot of makeup since losing sixteen pounds over the summer—a consequence of going to the Sophomore Blowout in June and having no one ask her to dance. That was at her old high school, in Bloomington. She had come home in tears and had confronted Stankowski and Beth in the living room. They were watching "Saturday Night Live." Irene shrieked that she was fat and Stankowski was fat and Beth was fat and Andy was fat. She announced that a hippopotamus could live in the family and no one would even notice. She said one of the boys at the dance had called her a flying cow.

The next night, Beth came home with sheaves of recipes from a Weight Watchers menu book. She had Xeroxed them. She and Irene dieted, and Andy, unbeknownst to anyone, instituted a diet himself in which he didn't eat anything for two days. Everyone thought he was sick. He came down with a severe case of nightmares, and eventually Stankowski got him to swallow a peanut-butter-and-jelly sandwich at two in the morning and to explain what was going on. After that, he was all right. Beth quit after a week and a half, but Irene kept going. One night as she rolled around in bed she discovered that she could open the screen in the window that was just beyond the end of her mattress and could stick her head out into the summer air. She could look up and see the stars burning. God, she thought, were they burning.

"She decided not to come," Stankowski said.

He was at his parents' house. He put the milk he'd bought into their refrigerator. He didn't know what else to say. He had just dropped off his father's lawn mower. He and Beth had bought a house but hadn't gotten around to buying a lawn mower yet. He stood in his mother's kitchen.

"I thought we had her. She wanted to go to the drugstore, and I figured we could get her over here to say hello."

"That's too bad," his mother said. "I was thinking of sewing her something. School's starting pretty soon."

Stankowski had his hands on the pantry counter and was looking out the back window. By the garage, his father and Andy were bent over the lawn mower. Andy was practically popping out of his pants. They'd played golf that morning and the kid had played very badly. A golf swing was too intricate, Stankowski thought; it took too long to learn and was too relentlessly, heartlessly unrewarding. He was bothered by a mental image he had of the boy waddling down the fairway like some kind of depressed piglet, sadly thumping the ground with his 3-wood. Andy was the only one of the family who was badly overweight. Stankowski was merely beefy—he had the shoulders and torso of some Great Plains ruminant, and his hair was cut across the back of his broad head midlevel at the ears. Far below, the seat of his pants sagged. "Don't sew her something," he said. "It's just not a good idea."

"You think she'd like it if I took her shopping?"

"I think she'd like to go shopping."

"But not with me."

Stankowski shrugged. "She's pretty bad company these days."

"I could go whether she likes it or not."

"You could."

Outside, Andy hauled on the starter cord and the mower coughed, then began to roar. Stankowski couldn't see his father's face and didn't know what he'd said, but the kid was smiling.

———

Beth got home at three-thirty and looked at the message board on the refrigerator. It said, BIGMOUTH CALL ROBERTA and MOM, DAD WILL BE RIGHT BACK HE'S AT QUIKMART TRYING TO FIND OUT WHO IRENE RAN OFF ON A HARLEY WITH.

Beth walked into the living room, her arms folded, and looked at the back of Andy's head. He was watching the Mets on television.

"What," he said.

"When did this happen?"

"Before. She got sick of waiting in the car."

"What's your father say?"

"He's mad. He said she hurt Grandma's feelings. He said she was supposed to at least say hi before she took off."

"So this was before you got to Grandma's?"

"When we got back home and she wasn't here, Dad said he'd see if she was at QuikMart. And when she wasn't there he said he'd see if she was at the drugstore. And when she wasn't there he said he'd see if the fat broad saw where they went."

Beth put her hand on Andy's head. She turned it halfway around.

"Don't talk like that. Are you worried about your sister?"

"No."

"Was it really a Harley?"

"Jesus," Andy said. "You think I don't know?"

At QuikMart, the clerk in blue sweatpants was stocking cigarettes. "I have smoked two packs today," she said. "I have smoked two packs. Those kids make me nervous."

Stankowski scuffed his feet.

"They all hang around the doughnut shop."

"Do you remember anything?" he asked.

"I remember two of them. They were calling me things."

The clerk walked to the rear of the store and opened a door by the milk coolers. Inside was a desk. There was a calendar on the wall which had a picture of three kittens spilling out of a hat. She consulted something scrawled on a notepad, copied it, ripped the sheet off, handed it to him. It was a license-plate number.

Stankowski took the paper and went out and sat in the pickup truck. He put the paper on the seat and put his elbows on either side of the yoke in the steering wheel and put his chin in his hands. He closed his eyes for a moment, then opened them. He was staring at the speedometer. *Miles per hour,* it said.

"Splat," Andy said. He had his fingers in his ears.

"He's not eating anything," Beth grumbled.

"Let him deal with this," Stankowski told her.

"I'm just not sure how to handle it."

Andy couldn't hear what anyone was saying, but he assumed it wasn't worth much. That was usually the case with this crowd. He was across the patio from his parents. Except for a few babies, he was the only one here who wasn't an adult. There were a couple of Japanese-from-California scientists and a few American scientists and a whole slew of British scientists. The guy who owned the condo was German. There had been scientists from all over the place in Seattle and Indiana, too. If you were a scientist and you didn't speak with an accent, you were practically a freak. Andy stopped thinking about scientists and started thinking about baseball—baseballs hit so far you could hardly see them anymore.

"Boom," he said. He crossed his arms over his stomach. Smoke from the barbecue was wafting by. It looked as if it was going to rain. He wondered if it was raining on the Mets.

Stankowski had owned a motorcycle once. It had been a Ducati and very fast. He remembered the dense, live weight of it, the streets shining in the rain, the vibrations like an electrical current running between his shoulder blades. He understood that there was a deep and potent connection between danger and love. That wasn't helping his composure much at the moment.

"I know where they are," he said. "They went to the beach."

Beth turned sideways, pushed her feet into the armrest of the couch, straining hard. Her face reddened. It was past midnight.

"Meigs Point. Hammonasset. Rocky Neck. They could have gone all the way to Rhode Island. It's just the usual stuff. Nightclubs, batting cages. Hamburger joints."

"Saturday Night Live" was on. Beth got up and turned it off. "I'm getting a little tired of having this on every time we have a crisis with her," she said. "How's she going to get home if it's raining?"

Stankowski was actually short of breath. A friend of his had been killed—literally beheaded—in a motorcycle accident. Stankowski, both timid and wild back then, had felt his internal balance tip after that. After that, he no longer trusted himself on two wheels. "Teenagers around here probably still do the same things," he said. "This place is in a time warp. It hasn't changed in twenty years."

"All the factories are empty."

"Yeah, but they look the same."

Genecorp, where Beth worked, was located in a renovated factory, an old steel-rolling mill now divided by felt-lined panels into offices, work stations, and biology laboratories. You had to use computer-coded cards to get through the doors. It didn't look the same at all. Beth worked with the enzyme Resolvase, which, as far as Stankowski understood it—and a biologist would have told him he didn't understand it very well—knitted up strands of DNA that were broken, deep within living cells, when jumping genes jumped from one place to another. Resolvase cleaned up molecular-biological messes.

"They're probably drinking," Stankowski said. "They roar off to one place, they roar off to another. It's dangerous. What can I tell you?"

"I kind of wish you'd shut up."

After a minute, Beth said, "I wonder what other little traditions they have on these beach trips?"

Stankowski didn't answer.

"They don't have to stop her. They just have to look for the license plate. If they see it, they can tell us where she is. They can tell us she's O.K."

"If we call the cops," Stankowski said, "she'll hate us for ten years."

"You don't have to tell me. I don't especially want

to call the cops. I know how that works. If you call the cops it turns out she's over at Roberta's, or it turns out she showed up at your mother's after all and they're playing Scrabble. But if you don't call the cops—if you don't embarrass yourself—then you feel like someone's going to pay for it. It's like you increase the chances that your daughter's splattered all over a bridge abutment."

"Jesus Christ!" Stankowski yelled.

"Sorry."

"Did you pick up this stuff from Andy? He's been talking like that all day." Stankowski stood up. "Look. They went to the beach. They can't get home because it's raining. Don't call the cops. Don't blow a fuse. Call it a night. If she's going to do this kind of thing, we're not going to wait up for her."

Beth got up from the couch. She gave a mock salute. There was a certain shift in control here; it happened occasionally.

"And whatever you do, when she comes back, don't ask her what she did."

"She won't tell us anyway."

The phone rang. "No, Roberta," Beth said into the receiver. "She can't come to the phone, and it's too late for this kind of calling."

Stankowski thought that at some point he would like to stay up all night for a cheerful reason. It hadn't happened when his children were born; they had arrived in each case while the sun was up. And the defining event of his life to date had been a nightlong ordeal. He had plummeted into the jungle in a helicopter when he was in the Army. In 1968 he had gone straight down into the trees outside Olongapo, in the Philippines, while he was taking blood supplies to a military hospital. His seat belt didn't work properly, and he smashed his face into the control panel and injured his back. He spent all night with one eye open, staring at the airspeed dial, with no feeling in his legs, waiting for someone to come and get him. It occurred to him as the hours passed that perhaps he was so low-profile that no one had noticed he was missing. It occurred to him as the hours passed that perhaps he wasn't the type who should willingly do spectacular things with his life. Later they operated on his back and fixed it, but they couldn't do much for his nose. Half of it didn't work, and now he received a small monthly disability check.

He sat up. It was three-thirty. Beth's eyes were open. She was staring at the ceiling. There were grunts coming from Andy's room. Stankowski got out of bed and went down the hall.

"You should have eaten something," he said.

"She thinks she's the only one who counts," Andy grumbled.

"We don't think that."

"She could get splatted all over the road."

"Andy!" Stankowski roared. Then he said, "Even if you diet, you've got to eat something. You don't eat nothing."

The boy was crying, and Stankowski looked away—directly into the face of the clock radio, which informed him that it was three thirty-seven.

"I liked her better when she was fat," Andy said.

Stankowski wondered if he could see his family disintegrating in the eerie, glowing progression of minutes and hours registered by the clock—see it the way you could see broken bones in X rays. He had a deep-seated fear that Beth was reevaluating, now that she had her Ph.D. and her career was taking off. He was afraid that she would be talking to him soon, explaining that for centuries *men* had been leaving *women*. She made twice as much money as he did, and when she socialized with her colleagues he couldn't even understand what they were talking about.

"How'd the Mets do today?" he asked.

"I only saw three innings. They were losing."

The phone rang and Stankowski froze. The sound jangled through the house, then ended abruptly as Beth answered in the bedroom. The door was open; he could hear her. "Yes," she said. Then, "Yes." Then, "What do you want us to do?" Then, "Great. What's wrong with you?"

Stankowski met her in the hallway.

"She's O.K.," Beth said, "but she's a long way off."

"You go."

"She doesn't want us. She said, 'I'm all right, this is boring, I'll be back when it stops raining.' They're at some Mexican restaurant in New London. It's closed for the night. They're standing under the eaves." Beth shook her head.

"So what's the story?"

"She said, 'Because it's the first time a boy's asked me to do anything.' "

"Wonderful."

In his room, Andy rolled over, played a drumroll on his stomach, stared at the ceiling. He heard his parents start to argue.

". . . go get her," Beth said. "I don't care what she thinks."

"I'm more worried about the kid in the other room."

"What's wrong with you? We've got a crisis here, and he's safe in his bed."

"He's not safe in his bed. He's miserable."

"Bill, she's fifty miles away in the middle of a monsoon."

"I know that. She has some big crisis every month and she gets a big reaction. He has a dozen little disasters every day and we practically ignore him."

Andy stared at the ceiling.

"He's so jealous he wants her to get into an accident," Stankowski said.

"So you don't think we should go?"

"No. She doesn't want us there. What're we going to do? Drag her away by the ankles?"

"That might not be necessary."

"You can't expect to rescue her every time she screws up."

"Well, this time we've got a chance."

"Look," Stankowski told her, "you've been running the family for the last ten years. Don't let me tell you what to do. If you want to go, go."

A door slammed. Andy began to cry again. Standing at the top of the stairs, Stankowski wished, not for the first time, that the enzyme Resolvase could be purified and marketed and used by people who weren't molecular biologists—that it could be sprinkled on average problems, to patch them up. There was nothing like that available, and so he was reduced to listening to the rain smashing onto the roof and talking with his son about a baseball team sunk far into last place.

He woke at two minutes after five. Andy was facedown on the bed. Stankowski was slouched in a chair with a hand on the boy's back, and Beth was standing over him. She was wearing a raincoat.

"She wasn't there," she said.

He stood up and they embraced. Her shoulders were shaking, but in sixteen years he had never seen her cry, and she wasn't crying now. They sat on the floor with their backs against the bed.

"This is thrilling, isn't it?" she said after a minute.

Gradually, a murky light filled the room and the boy snored and Stankowski found himself dreading some nebulous, gray fate as a divorced man who hung around doughnut shops. "Can't," he mumbled.

"What?" Beth barked, waking him up.

At seven-ten, the police came. Stankowski snapped his eyes open, woke up again. He'd dreamed that, too. His stomach had the unfettered, ballooning sensation one got from plunging through the air, and there was an intense roaring, the sound of a fleet of helicopters or of the sun landing and burning in the front yard. It had stopped raining, and the early light was already hot. Stankowski got up and looked out the window and saw four motorcycles in the road. The boys looked almost familiar; with longer hair, they might have been his friends from twenty years ago. There was a young woman tumored to the back of one of the motorcycles, looking cold and lethargic, and then Stankowski saw Irene on the lawn. She waved her arms as if beating off flies.

"Get lost!" she howled. *"You're waking everyone up!"*

Irene took off a green sweatshirt—Stankowski guessed someone had given it to her—and walked over the grass, shaking her head, tapping an ear with a palm. The noise faded. The street was quiet. The sun hit her hair.

"You all right?" he called.

Irene cast a tired, corrosive glance up at the second story of the house. She still wore her shorts and white blouse. They looked damp but unsullied. She leaned against the pickup truck and, tapping her ears, seemed surprised to find earrings.

"God," she said. "I thought they were blown off. You ever been locked in a room with four hundred chain saws?"

"You ever been locked in a room for two months for scaring the hell out of your parents?"

"Oh, great. You guys are going to nail me for this, and it wasn't even fun. It wasn't even worth it."

She took off the earrings, pulled a hair ribbon from a pocket, tossed these things sarcastically over her shoulder into the back of the pickup. "Go ahead," she said. "Wreck the rest of my summer."

Since yesterday, the sunlight had gone softer,

Stankowski thought—less acid, more golden, as if summer were finally turning to fall. But that didn't quite describe what he was feeling. It was more of an internal shift. When a potential disaster failed to come off—however likely or unlikely—you were apt to get some kind of small, positive jolt in spite of yourself. Things weren't actually better, but briefly they looked that way. It was a little early for a beer, but Stankowski found he wanted one. It seemed to him that the image of beer bottles sweating at the back of the refrigerator on a hot day, coupled with the relief he was feeling at the moment, were about as close to Resolvase as he was going to get.

H O B E R

SUPERIOR MUFFLERS was on Sharpe Avenue, not far from the Mobil gasoline-storage tanks. The tanks fronted on Thayer Street, which ran from I-91 to the rail yard by the old Helio Thread plant, where last week there had been a gang-related drive-by shooting. According to Hober's girlfriend, dragons hung around there—she claimed the city turned into Camelot in the middle of the night. A castle appeared downtown, she said, next to the Kennedy public-housing project.

Hober's son was suspended from school again—he had thrown a cigarette at a teacher—and Hober was getting the news a day late, over the phone, and looking out the rear windows of the office. The fuel tanks were indistinct, because it was snowing. "In the forehead?" he said. He turned and saw that Blunschi, who specialized in finding muffler parts at discount, was smirking at him. "Today doesn't count," Hober said. "It's a holiday. If he's got three days off for bad behavior, that's Friday, Monday, and Tuesday . . . I don't know, next time I see him. You guys should've blasted him one already. If he pulls something like that, he should be too scared to come into the house." Hober's voice was hoarse; he'd caught a virus. He was talking to Raylene, his ex-wife.

He and Blunschi had expected the call to be someone cancelling a repair. The snow had been falling since early morning. Now the roads were bad. It was Veterans Day. So far, six of the twelve jobs scheduled for the afternoon had been called off; people didn't want to drive their cars in. Blunschi and Hober owned Superior Mufflers, along with Joe Callebas.

Hober went out into the sound-deadened air at noon and wiped the snow from his windshield. There was no sign of plowing or sanding on Sharpe Avenue. Across from the muffler shop was Bess Eaton Donuts, which seemed to be hosting a convention of four-wheel-drive pickup trucks. If the storm kept up, snowmobiles would be out later, when it was dark—there were quite a few in town, considering that the place was almost entirely covered with buildings and asphalt and hadn't had a serious winter in five years.

Hober's girlfriend, Tracy Robards, who was a nurse at Community Hospital, had rented *Camelot* in August from Video Kid. Seeing it for the first time in twenty-five years, she had laughed and danced around her apartment to the music. "Loopy!" she kept yelling. "This movie is loopy!" In September, the other nurses on Three West had signed her up for the Fall Makeover Lottery—part of the hospital auxiliary's annual fashion show. Her name was picked in the drawing, and after the fashion show and the photo display on the cafeteria bulletin board, Tracy went to New Haven and bought all the clothes the consultant had selected for her. She spent twenty-four hundred dollars and had to cancel a trip to Martinique she had planned for February with two nursing friends. After hanging up the clothes and putting the new shoes away, Tracy was extremely unhappy. That lasted several weeks. These days, she was still disproportionately angry about the hair style Modern Mode had given her, but otherwise seemed all right. Hober liked her hair. He thought it looked as if she had stuck her finger in an electric-light socket.

Hober drove to Thorpe Street, halted his Subaru in front of his grandparents' house, and began to clear their sidewalk with the muffler shop's plastic-bladed shovel. He coughed occasionally, and as he bent and stood it felt as if a load of wet cement were shifting around inside his head. The houses here were about a hundred years old. There were large maples between the street and the walk, and their roots had tilted a number of the slates. The air was full of snow. Hober wore a blue mechanic's jacket, zipped to the neck against the weather, matching blue pants, and a knit cap of highway-safety orange. The jacket had a trim cut. Hober was five feet seven and thin, and his movements, except when he was fumbling for a Kleenex, were birdlike or military.

"Stu wrecked his car," he told his grandparents at lunch. There was no other family news he wanted to pass along. He was eating soup. Stu was his older brother, and the accident was an embarrassment: Stu taught driver education at Kroeber State Technical School. Also, he had been drunk. Hober didn't go into that. For that matter, he wasn't sure that Henry and Renee Fleury, his maternal grandparents, knew that Stu's wife had moved out in August. "He was backing out of Cumberland Farms and got hit by a truck," he said. "Failure to grant right-of-way."

Conversation about Hober's business had to be kept brief and vague, although Henry Fleury, a retired silver-factory executive, always asked about it with interest. Superior Mufflers survived on what Hober called "the catalytic-converter factor." There was no easy way for Hober to explain to his grandfather that he and his partners were willing to weld muffler pipe closer to the converters than the Midas shops were willing to risk. A small business such as Superior was less likely to be inspected by the state; it was able to underbid. Word got around. Also, Hober had worked for the Highway Department and for DeLorea Construction, and Blunschi had been a mechanic at DeLorea; they knew people. Not necessarily by competitive bidding, they got to do a lot of general repairs on city vehicles and on the construction and maintenance trucks DeLorea leased to the state.

"There are so many cars and so many bays to put them in," Hober said to Henry.

When Renee, his grandmother, issued her usual request for Ricky to visit, Hober explained that the boy was in trouble and wouldn't be socializing for a while. Ricky, who was twelve, almost never came to see the Fleurys.

Henry asked, "Do you think he'd come if I said I had a hole in my head?"

"What?"

"I was sick on this day in 1918. Exactly. The first Armistice. My father took my mastoid bone out."

Hober had never heard anything about a mastoid bone. After a minute, Henry bent his bald head forward. He reached across the table and took Hober's hand and placed it behind his right ear. There was a pouch there. The skin was as wrinkled and soft as old felt. The dining room had tall windows with lace curtains that were almost transparent, and now the gray day entered the room. Hober felt ill and thickheaded—going from the sharp air outside to the warm, stuffy interior of the house was a rough transition for someone with a ripe, early cold. His left index finger was fishhooked half an inch into his grandfather's skull. The heat coming from Henry's head surprised Hober; it was partly the contrast with his cold hands, but he also thought of the hot skin of a baby—Henry was practically as bald. After a moment, Hober began to think more clearly—clearly enough, at least, to know that he wanted a cigarette. And he couldn't have one until he left.

"This was before antibiotics," Henry said, sitting up.

After a moment Hober felt behind his own ear, touching a bone that was like the curving earpiece of a pair of glasses.

"At the end of World War One, the swine flu killed twenty million people in four months," Henry said.

"That's twice as many as the war killed in four years. I was eight years old. I got it in November. Then I developed some kind of secondary infection, probably bacterial. My father thought the bone was involved. The bone's porous. If the infection goes through that to the brain, it kills you."

Henry explained what had happened. Many doctors and nurses had fallen ill during the flu epidemic. His father, Arthur Fleury, was in bed at the time with a high fever. He waited for two days, then decided that if he waited any longer he might be too ill to perform the operation or Henry too weak to survive it. He took his son to the office, put him under with ether, and sawed out the mastoid bone on the morning of the Armistice.

"My father went home to bed around noon," Henry went on. "He had to push his way through the people who were dancing in the streets. Other people were shooting guns off. I went to the St. Regis rectory on a stretcher. It didn't matter if you were Catholic or Protestant by then—all the hospital beds were full. There was an infirmary set up at the high school, but that was full, too. I was at the rectory with six or seven others. There was no morphine. I wanted to sleep, but the church was next door and they were ringing the bell all day long to celebrate the Armistice. Every time the bell rang, I thought my head was going to explode."

Henry's only sibling, George, a younger brother, had died of pneumonia in 1915, which meant that on that Armistice Day Arthur Fleury was facing the prospect that he might soon be childless. As it turned out, Arthur died the following week, and Henry was left fatherless.

Renee, who had grown up in Springfield, Massachusetts, said that her sister, Elizabeth Willis, aged six, had died of the flu on November 8, 1918, three days before Arthur saved Henry's life.

"I've got to get back to work," Hober said. He tried, a little groggily, to remember how Henry had gotten onto this subject, which was so far from what they usually talked about that they might have been discussing Martians. Hober also wondered if there was some message involved, such as that he and Ricky weren't living up to their ancestors.

"Sit down," Henry told him.

Later that afternoon, Hober was on the phone, telling Nancy Ortek to pick up her car at four-thirty instead of three-thirty. Nancy was a nurse-practitioner at MedServ. Everyone in the shop knew her; their health insurance required them to go there. Also, she was a friend of Tracy's. Hober had started work on Nancy's muffler, but then Blunschi had taken over, because Hober's head was bothering him. Three more jobs had been cancelled. It was a slow afternoon. Blunschi was taking his time with Nancy's Honda, and now he had gone across the street for coffee.

Shortly after hanging up, Hober got a call from George DeLorea, of DeLorea Construction, who wanted him to drive a snowplow all night. The storm hadn't ended at noon, as predicted. "The city's caught with its pants down," DeLorea said. "I want to make some money out of this."

Hober worked Saturdays—partners at Superior Mufflers put in six-day weeks. The rule about calling in sick, as defined by Callebas, was that you could do it if you were dead. Callebas and Hober and Blunschi rarely took vacation days, either. They referred to this as the "Jap approach." Hober didn't want to drive a plow all night and then work all day Friday and then from seven to noon on Saturday. On the other hand, he owed De-Lorea, who once had given him a job and now sent regular business to the shop, and he owed Joe Venturi, the Highway Department superintendent. "If Joe's that desperate, tell him to call me himself," he said. It was the same as giving in.

Superior Mufflers sat diagonally on its lot. Once it had been Krasner Oil. In the rear corner of the lot was Hober's brother's Camry, its back side severely crumpled from its collision. Beyond the fence to the west was a three-decker house of the sort Blunschi called a "Polish battleship." Two little Hispanic girls lived there. Earlier, they had been outside, in matching pink snowsuits, building a pair of snowmen by the sidewalk. A group of older kids, off school for the holiday and walking back from the mall, had stopped later on and molested the snowmen in some way.

Around three-thirty, Tracy called to see what Hober was doing for dinner, and Hober ended up relating what Henry Fleury had told him. "So if my great-grandfather hadn't deboned Henry," he said, "I wouldn't be here."

"I don't know," Tracy told him. "That stuff gets confusing. Maybe a quarter of you wouldn't be here, and three-quarters would. One-quarter would be different."

"I'd own one-quarter less than one-third of the muffler shop."

In Hober's thirty-seven years—or the thirty or so when he might have been capable of understanding family history—he had never visited his grandfather on November 11th. Henry had kept track. Nor had Stu, nor had any of the Fleurys' four other grandchildren. Grandchildren were spread from Boston to Seattle; there was little chance any would be in Connecticut, let alone at Thorpe Street, on Veterans Day. It wasn't a holiday when people travelled long distances to visit. Hober didn't visit the Fleurys except to shovel snow or to mow the grass, and it rarely snowed in early November. As Hober was leaving after lunch, Henry had tried to lend him a book, and Hober had grumbled, "Give it to Stu. He's the family schoolmarm." Before putting it back, his grandfather had pointed out a few things in the volume (it was Paul Fussell's *The Great War and Modern Memory*), including references to the sarcastic songs sung by the soldiers in the trenches, who quickly had realized that they were sacrificial parts in a huge machine whose only purpose was wholesale death. On one occasion, Henry said, a British battalion attacked with eight hundred men, and the next day only eighty were left. The phrases "over the top," "rank and file," and "no man's land," and the trenchcoat, and the current uses of the words "lousy" and "crummy," and the creation of daylight-saving time, and widespread cigarette smoking, and the regular use of wristwatches all dated from the war. Then the swine flu had come along.

Hober had the flu himself, it turned out. When

Nancy Ortek came to get her car, she put her hand against his forehead, then shoved him into one of the four plastic chairs lined up against the panelled wall of the office and waiting room. She got one of the muffler shop's greasy flashlights and shone it in his mouth and ears. "There's a little fever," she said. "Go home to bed. You're producing a lot of fluid."

"Snot," Hober told Callebas. "She means snot."

Shortly after that, Nancy got into an argument with Blunschi. Blunschi had removed the catalytic converter from her Accord. He said the car was so beat up that she'd have to scrap it long before its next emissions test.

"You're turning me into a crook!" she yelled.

"That car won't last six months. You want to send it to the junkyard with a new converter and a lot of new pipe?"

"You could've been legal. I would've paid."

"You remind me of Margaret in 'Dennis the Menace,' " Blunschi said angrily. "Follow the rules. Be a good boy. Don't smoke in the boys' room. *I'm telling.*" Blunschi returned to the garage to take the car off the lift.

"He doesn't do that for everybody," Hober said. He was making out the bill.

"I hate stuff like that."

"Well, that's what makes the world go round around here."

"Why do people say that? *'That's what makes the world go round.'* They make it sound like the world actually works."

"This isn't like murdering somebody," Hober told her. "He's helping you out. It wasn't worth the money."

"He's trying to get me into trouble."

"What do you think's going to happen? Someone's going to keep you after school?"

A few minutes later, Hober and Blunschi went out into the snow to see Nancy off. Blunschi followed as far as the street. "You criminal!" he yelled as she drove off. "Felon! I'm calling the cops!" Something about the snowmen next door distracted him, and he went to take a closer look. "That's nice," he said when he came back. "One says 'Fuck' and the other says 'You.' Across the chests in gravel."

"I don't think the little girls did that."

When they returned to the office, Callebas had just picked up the phone. He handed the receiver to Hober. It was Venturi, the highway superintendent. "Where's your loyalty to the goddam city?" Venturi asked. "I got three of my drivers deer hunting in New Hampshire. I can't even get in touch with them."

That wasn't all. Venturi went on to say that the city Purchasing Department had waited until the new fiscal quarter began in October before ordering plows for five new trucks that had been delivered over the summer. The plows hadn't arrived. The old plows didn't fit the new trucks. Three older trucks had been sold. Two others were sitting in the city garage, but the insurance on them had lapsed. Venturi had tried calling the municipal cooperative to reinstate the coverage, but the office was closed for Veterans Day.

Hober agreed to plow snow with one of DeLorea's Macks, starting at seven-thirty.

There was a standard local physique. A number of men around town stashed their excess weight high on the torso—at midchest and around the shoulder blades. They might have had inner tubes grafted below the armpits. Tracy said they looked like Michelin men with half the air sucked out of them. The buttocks were apt to be small—comparatively, anyway. Hober saw a silhouette like that as he was driving home—it was stumping along Sharpe Avenue through the gloom by the long-abandoned Bantam Specialty Steel mill, and it took an instant for him to realize that it was his brother.

There was a miniplaza in front of the factory, with a dry cleaner's, a pizzeria, and a QuikMart, and Hober veered toward the parking lot. Once he was out of the two ruts that served for westbound traffic, the car took a more oblique line than he had intended; he twisted the wheel farther to the right, and the rear of the car swung around, hopped the curb, and hit a light pole.

Hober turned off the engine. He noticed that his pulse was thudding dully—it sounded as if somewhere inside the factory a large machine were still stamping out metal sheets. Dark had fallen and headlights were on; snowflakes came down like Styrofoam packing pellets. The car had ricocheted a couple of feet from the pole and was more or less sideways to the road. Three wheels were on the sidewalk. Hober blew his nose and watched through the windshield as a woman dashed from the dry cleaner's across the road to a car she'd left in the Kentucky Fried Chicken lot. She paused for a moment and stared at Hober's Subaru with open-mouthed, impersonal curiosity, as if it were something on television, then went on, splashing in the gutter.

When Stu rapped on the window, Hober looked at him balefully and threw open the door. The air was full of snow.

"What the hell was that all about? I *thought* that was you."

"How'd you like it?" Hober asked.

"It was great. This bunch of cars goes by and then suddenly one of them breaks out of line, heads off at an angle, and smashes into a pole."

"If you didn't look like a goddam werewolf, I wouldn't've recognized you and this never would have happened," Hober said angrily.

"What'd you stop for?"

"Because you're a basket case. If I see you wandering around in the middle of a snowstorm, I figure there's some kind of problem."

The left-rear fender was crumpled against the tire, which had gone flat. Hober supposed he could pry out the metal with the crowbar he kept in his trunk, then crawl around in the slush and put on the spare, but something cockeyed about the way the car was sitting made him realize there was no point—he'd bent the axle or the wheel hub when he banged against the curb.

Stu was wearing an Oakland Raiders windbreaker. His hair and shoulders were covered with wet snow. He said he'd just visited the cash machine at Home Dime.

"You couldn't take the driver's-ed car?"

"I'm not pushing my luck."

Stu was allowed to bring the driver's-ed Chevy home from his job at Kroeber Tech, but he wasn't supposed to use it for personal business.

Stu had been lucky Tuesday night—he hadn't been injured or killed, despite being clobbered by the tractor-trailer. Also, the cop who had showed up to deal with the accident was a friend of his, Larry Wisch. Wisch hadn't administered the test obviously called for. While it wasn't a good thing for a driver's-ed teacher to cause an accident, it was a disaster if he was charged with D.W.I.

From a pay phone by the rest rooms in Greek God Pizza, Hober called the muffler shop. No answer— Blunschi and Callebas had gone. Hober studied the nicks in the panelling of the telephone nook. Along with the usual obscenities, he saw "Tigres" and "Hood Boyzz," the names of local gangs. After a minute, he made another call and ordered a tow truck from Mike Cavullo at Mid-State Garage. Then he reached Tracy at home and asked her to drive over. "We'll have to eat here," he said. "Then I need a ride across town." They had planned to have dinner at her apartment, but De-Lorea's equipment yard was over on the west side, and there wasn't time.

After hanging up, he went into the main part of the restaurant. There were no other customers. The couple who ran the place had colonized the booth by the counter; a small TV was there, tuned to a "Happy Days" episode—no one watching—and several plastic toys lay on the padded bench. A toddler banged around in the aisle with a stroller while his mother mowed at the red carpet with a vacuum cleaner. Hober, his head awash, felt acutely the season and the hour: November, probably the ugliest month of the year; early evening, the time of sitcom reruns and roaring appliances. He had the sense that everyone else in the city was either comfortably home or on the way home, happily avoiding the kind of foul-up that had just happened to him. He ordered a large pepperoni pizza and joined Stu in a booth by the window.

"You better stick around for a while," Hober said. "I've got to leave in forty minutes. If the tow truck doesn't come by then, you can be here when it shows up. This is your goddam fault anyway." With his sleeve, he swabbed rheumily at the mist on the window. He was looking for Cavullo.

"What's the story with the Fleurys?" Stu asked. "They said they saw you this afternoon. They practically ordered me to come to dinner. They're not usually like that. There's stuff I'd rather do with my evenings."

"Like what? The Lamplighter Lounge?"

This was a fairly crude reference to the collapse of Stu's marriage. The Lamplighter Lounge, out on the Franey Turnpike, reputedly was jammed on weekends with fiftyish divorcées with bouffant hairdos and men the same age wearing sports jackets over shirts unbuttoned down to the navel.

"Shut up," Stu told him. He was looking out the window. Then he turned and said, "That looks great."

Hober had a balled-up Kleenex rammed into one nostril. He lit a cigarette, taking care to keep the flame away from the Kleenex. Over the next few minutes the two brothers filled the air with smoke.

Hober said, "The old guy's going to talk your ear off. I've never seen him like that. He wanted the little porker to visit, but I told him the little porker's grounded. He got suspended again."

"The little porker came over Sunday night when it was pouring," Stu said. "He was using one of his schoolbooks for an umbrella. *Adventures in Reading*. Is that why he's in trouble? He was holding it on top of his head. It was a great idea—the thing's the size of home plate. But I bet the pages swelled up like pancakes."

Ricky often came by Stu's, because he had a free rein with Stu's television. There was more competition at home from Ricky's mother, Raylene, and from her husband, Jeff Paquette. They lived on the other side of Cote Hill from Stu.

"Little porker threw his cigarette at a teacher in the main hall of Grasso Junior High," Hober said.

"Lit?"

"Probably. Raylene didn't say the guy was burned—just insulted. But it was probably lit."

After twenty minutes, Hober saw flashing lights through the window, and he and Stu went outside. Mike Cavullo had sent his son, Jimmy, who was thin and wore nothing against the snow but a white T-shirt. The truck was old and green, and said "Mid-State Garage" in gold letters on the main span of the derrick. When the Subaru had been hoisted by the rear, Hober told Jimmy through the open window of the cab, "Dump it at the shop, next to Fuckhead here's Camry."

"Maybe we should shoot for three in a row," Stu said as Jimmy drove off down Sharpe Avenue. "Get the Fleurys to wreck their Model T, or whatever it is they're driving these days."

"You're a barrel of laughs."

Stu hulked around on the sidewalk, throwing snowballs at the light pole and at the Dumpster in the corner of the lot, by the convenience store. "You know the little porker's textbook?" he asked. "I didn't know they still did that. I remember when we were kids they used to call everything 'adventure' this, 'adventure' that. Anything really boring, it was an adventure. *Adventures in Reading, Adventures in Mathematics.* I think I was twenty-five before I figured out 'adventure' didn't mean 'boring.'"

Hober heaved a snowball toward a mailbox on the next corner, but it fell short. The traffic along Sharpe Avenue was heavy and moving slowly.

"I don't mind paying money if somebody'll get off his butt and actually fix my car," Stu said. "You guys don't usually do bodywork. If you're too busy, just say so, and I'll take it somewhere else. I got insurance."

"You won't get no skim job if you do that," Hober told him. "Be patient. We'll get around to it, charge four thousand, spend three thousand, split the difference. Where the hell's Tracy?"

"Probably cracked up. Why'd you ask her to drive in this stuff?"

Hober was getting fed up with his brother. "Do me a favor," he said. "When you're done with dinner at the old-folks home over there, shovel the sidewalk. How come I'm the only one who ever helps those guys out?

I already did it once today. Where the hell were you? You had the day off. You work for the goddam *state*."

Hober was repeating an epithet often heard when he'd worked for DeLorea Construction. Callebas still used it whenever events at the muffler shop got on his nerves. "Screw this," he'd say. "I'm gonna work for the *state*."

A few minutes later a silver hatchback pulled into the lot, and Tracy got out. Stu said hello and ended up coming inside for a slice of pizza before walking over to the Fleurys' for dinner.

DeLorea was right: the city was caught with its pants down. As Hober banged around that evening in the beat-up truck DeLorea had given him, the dashboard C.B.-radio scanner often stopped on the Highway Department band, otherwise known as the "snow channel," or, after Venturi's nickname during storms, the "Little Miss Snowflake Channel." Policemen, nettled by the numerous accidents and by the nuisance of skidding and wallowing around in the glop, showed up at the city garage one after another, demanding snow tires. Their cruisers weren't prepared for winter. That delayed repairs to a plow Venturi had been counting on, which had a broken oil pump. Later the cops wanted chains, and some of the chains didn't fit—five cruisers bought over the last two years had fatter tires than the other cruisers, including some also bought over the same period. The cars in most specifics were the same, and it took a while to figure out which were affected and which weren't. Meanwhile, the construction-company drivers radioed in questions about plowing routes, and even some of the Highway Department regulars weren't sure where they were going. Photocopied maps had been given out, but they were small and hard to read in the half-lit cabs of the trucks. Nothing could be done about parked cars, because the city's winter-towing ordinance didn't take effect until November 15th.

Hober's truck didn't steer well, the heater put out rancid, stale air, and the rumbling of the plow seemed to go straight through his swollen sinuses to the bones in his cheeks. DeLorea had five Macks and G.M.C.s on the road, and was driving the oldest of the G.M.C.s himself. Contractors used older equipment for plowing because plowing caused a lot of wear and tear. Hober was familiar with his route—it was in the northeast section of the city—and that was a help. Through the windshield, the world looked light and insubstantial, and when he sneezed his head ballooned in and out and the thirteen tons around him briefly turned weightless. He and the truck floated like two snowflakes among millions of others.

When he turned down Thorpe Street, shortly before midnight, he couldn't tell whether Stu had shovelled out the Fleurys, but it was clear someone would have to excavate them again in the morning. Several cars were parked along the curb, and Hober sluiced them in snow as if he were packing trench walls around bodies. Then he saw snow puffs drifting from the white willow tree in the Fleurys' side yard. He had mowed the lawn a couple of years ago on Memorial Day, and remembered the tree spewing its seed in the breeze as if there were a summer blizzard. Henry and Renee had come back from the cemetery as he was finishing— probably they'd been visiting Arthur's grave. Renee was holding a trowel and an empty pot she'd used for transporting flowers. The snowflakes now veering before the windshield were huge and sparse. The storm finally ended at twelve-thirty; there was a foot on the ground.

For some time in the patter of police calls there was discussion, with occasional angry comments from Venturi, about an accident between a plow and a snowmobile, no injuries. It was around one in the morning. The phrase "plow and snowmobile, no injuries" came over the radio several times and degenerated in Hober's mind into "cheese and pepperoni, no mushrooms," which he repeated nonsensically, as if it were the chorus to a song.

"You better get over here," DeLorea told him eventually, on the company channel. "Corner of Cote and Iris." Hober thought one of DeLorea's trucks must be involved.

There was a collection of twinkling lights atop Cote Hill: blue and a firecrackerish pink from two police cruisers, red and white from an ambulance, yellow from Venturi's battered Highway Department car. DeLorea's truck was parked at the curb, and Doug Muencher's G.M.C., evidently the truck that had been in the accident, sat diagonally in the front yard of the house at the southeast corner. It looked odd there. Cote Hill Road ran along the crest of the hill, while Iris went steeply up one side and down the other.

When Hober climbed down from his Mack, Muencher came over. He was a beefy man in a down vest. "That kid, he was spinning around in the snow," he said. A policeman came over to give Muencher a drunk-driving test, and then Venturi walked up and began to yell at the officer about snowmobiles. "I complain about this every year! You guys never do nothing! I'm surprised this didn't happen ten times already!"

"Listen, Little Miss Snowflake," the cop said. "We're as tired as you are. Shut up."

He asked Muencher if he had slowed for the intersection. "No," Muencher said. "You think I'm crazy? There's no stop sign. It's one o'clock in the morning. I've got five hundred pounds of snow on the plow. If I slip off somewhere and get stuck at the top of that hill, I'll be there the rest of the night."

Venturi asked, "For Christ's sake, did the kid slow down? *He's* got a stop sign. He's not even legal. Who lets his kid do something like that at one o'clock in the morning?"

Hober suddenly understood why he'd been called. He let the three men argue and looked around until he located the snowmobile. It was lodged sideways in a hedge on the far side of the next yard down, on Cote Hill Road. A policeman was looking at it, along with a man wearing pajamas, a bathrobe, and galoshes—apparently the homeowner. It turned out that he was the one who had identified Ricky. He had called him "the Paquette kid," and when Muencher reported this to DeLorea, DeLorea radioed Hober. Now Hober got close enough to the snowmobile to see that it looked like Stu's old red Polaris. He didn't know what kind of snowmobile Jeff Paquette owned. There was no sign of Ricky.

"Where is he?" he asked when Muencher was done with the drunk-driving test.

"He took off."

"Did he hit the truck?"

"Naw, he'd be dead then. I swerved, and I think he bounced off the snow in front of the plow. He must've been going thirty or forty. He went through that yard there and hit that bush and got bucked off. Snowmobile kept going. I went over to see if he was all right, and he was spinning around in the snow. After about thirty seconds he stops and looks up at me and says, 'Shit.' Then he tries to run away. I grab him, but he keeps trying to get loose. After the guy told me who he was, I just let him go. He was a chubby kid. Big butt."

"Jesus Christ almighty," Hober said.

"I guess I called the ambulance for nothing."

Hober spoke to the two policemen. He said he was the father and offered to visit the Paquettes. Ricky's last name wasn't Paquette, but Hober didn't go into that. As he climbed back into his truck, DeLorea came up and asked if Muencher could take it over. Muencher's truck wasn't damaged, but the police wanted it to stay put until they were done with their investigation. De-Lorea didn't want two plows off the clock if he could help it. Hober ended up getting a ride from Venturi to Sand Trap Lane, where the Paquettes lived.

After Venturi dropped him off, Hober rang the bell until Jeff Paquette woke up and let him in. They found Ricky in bed with a swollen wrist. Wet clothes were heaped on the floor.

"You think you were going to get away with this?" Paquette yelled, taking a few roundhouse swings as the boy struggled to get out of the blankets.

"Shit!" Ricky yelled. "Cut it out!"

Paquette was wearing an undershirt that hung loosely over his potbelly, and blue boxer shorts. He was in his mid-thirties and worked at the Mohr traprock quarry. He had a tattoo of a snake on his left forearm. He said Ricky had sneaked out—he wasn't supposed to leave the house until his school suspension was over, the following Wednesday. Once Raylene had got up, it was decided that Hober would borrow Raylene's car and take Ricky to the emergency room on the way to the police station. The boy's wrist was very swollen, and Raylene thought it might be broken.

"You're a complete fucking moron," Hober told Stu over the phone while Ricky got dressed. "That kid was grounded."

"I forgot," Stu said. "I was beginning to wonder if I should call someone. He was here when I got back from the Fleurys. The deal was he'd be back by midnight. I figured it was just the usual thing—he was on the other side of town or he made it to the golf course or he was halfway to Massachusetts."

As Hober followed the boy down the front steps, he turned and told Raylene he'd phone from the hospital.

"Just bring him back," she said. She wore a bathrobe. She appeared angry with Stu, but Hober told her Stu hadn't known there was a problem. Ricky had borrowed Stu's Polaris once or twice before, and the Paquettes hadn't objected.

211

When the door was shut, Hober turned and saw his son sitting in the snow that covered the sidewalk. Suddenly Ricky keeled over onto his side and began to make a paddling motion with his hands and feet. It looked like something a mechanical toy or a frustrated cat might do. He had snow all over his clothes and face and didn't seem to notice. Hober waded in, clubbing at him, trying to get him to stop. "What the hell's wrong with you?" he yelled. The chubby body spun with remarkable force—arresting it was like trying to tackle a pig. Hober got clipped across the shins and knocked half over, and he braced himself by sinking one hand into the fresh snow on the lawn. The grass at the bottom felt brittle and strange. By now the boy had halted and was struggling to sit up. "Fuck," he said, staring at his wrist.

Hober hauled him to his feet and propelled him toward the car. Along the way, he beat the snow off the back of his son's coat. A few minutes later, when they halted at the intersection of Iris and Cote Hill Road, Hober pointed at the stop sign and asked, "Ever seen one of those before?" Then he hit the boy so hard that his palm and fingers, only now recovering from the snow, went numb again. It was a slap rather than a punch, and Ricky's head banged against the passenger-side window. "Don't say nothing," Hober told him. "Don't say a word."

They turned from Sharpe Avenue onto Main, past a small Veterans Day reviewing stand that had been set up next to the war monuments. It held a number of metal folding chairs whose seats were covered with snow. No one had bothered to remove them. Then they turned onto Trencher and came to the hospital.

Hober met Tracy and Stu the next day at noon, at McDonald's. The sun ricocheted off the snow and blasted from windshields in the parking lot. The temperature was in the fifties. Hober and Stu needed to discuss what to tell the cops, and Tracy was there because Hober needed to borrow her car—he was supposed to drive Ricky over to see Youth Officer Ronald Jagowicz at one-fifteen. Hober's Subaru was still out of commission. He had returned Raylene's car on the way to work.

Raylene had picked up Ricky that morning, when he was released from the hospital. He had been kept there overnight for observation. He had started spinning in circles again in the emergency room, at two-thirty in the morning, while the doctor was examining him; the doctor and Hober had broken the boy's fall from the examining table to the floor as best they could. The physician told Hober that the spinning was a symptom of a concussion—a rare one. Apparently, it was caused by swelling in the part of the brain that controlled basic body movements. The boy wasn't really conscious when he had a spell like that. He wasn't exactly unconscious, either. He couldn't keep himself from doing it.

A neurologist was called in, and later Hober saw two nurses strap his son into a bed in the children's ward on the fourth floor. He lay plumply under the green blanket and white sheet, and immediately fell asleep. A nurse was going to wake him up every hour or so to make sure he hadn't blacked out. They didn't want to give him any painkilling drugs because of the concussion. The neurologist said there might be more

213

spinning episodes, although they would probably cease as the swelling receded. Ricky wore a plastic removable cast; he had a broken bone in his wrist.

While Ricky was visiting Youth Officer Jagowicz in the afternoon, Hober would see the desk sergeant, Raymond DeFrances, who would book him on a charge of third-degree assault. The E.R. physician had reported him for child abuse. That was after Hober, hearing that the boy had a concussion, had remarked, "I guess I shouldn't have smacked him one on the way to the hospital." The doctor said that if Hober had hit his son with a baseball bat it might have been worse. Otherwise, it was hard to imagine anything more abusive than giving a boy who had a concussion a hard slap on the side of the head.

Sergeant DeFrances was on Hober's side. When Hober had phoned that morning to arrange things, De-Frances told him it was unlikely the police would press charges. "If my kid pulled something like that," he said, "I'd knock his head clean off."

McDonald's was a few hundred yards down Sharpe Avenue from Superior Mufflers. An electric carillon in the Pentecostal church beyond the Video Kid was playing an irritating midday collection of hymns, and the notes tinkled through the window of the corner booth where they were sitting. Then a truck full of Domino's Pizza ingredients backfired as it halted in the traffic outside the restaurant, and Hober and Stu and Tracy jumped. The intense blue of the sky seemed to increase Hober's headache. He kept holding his paper coffee cup against his eyebrows and cheekbones.

"This family's really gone downhill," Stu said. "We got a doctor in our ancestry. I never knew that. Henry was the vice-president of a company, Mom and Dad were teacher-administrator hacks." Hober's parents had retired two years ago and moved to Vermont; his father had been the head of the high-school Guidance Department, and his mother had been the curriculum supervisor for the city's elementary schools. "I'm a driver-ed teacher who's asking to get fired, you're a grease monkey, and your kid's headed straight for prison."

"I'm part owner of a company," Hober said with irritation.

"Your grandfather's old company—you know, that's completely gone," Tracy said. "I was thinking about that. There's nobody left who worked for it except an old man here and there. It closed up twenty years ago. Then it burned down. Cook & Church was around for a hundred years, and now it's like it never happened."

"Didn't Henry's story get to you at all?" Stu asked Hober.

"It's more the sort of thing that would get to you, Stu."

"Well, you're a pissball. I was over there for dinner, and Henry came out with all this stuff about his father and the flu and World War One and everything, and at the end of it he was crying. Renee and I are patting him on the back, and he's bent over the dining-room table and he's got tears coming off the end of his nose. I think Henry's getting a little close to the finish line. Then, when I'm going out the door, Renee tells me you weren't even interested in hearing it."

"That's right," Hober said. "I needed a cigarette, I was sick, I figured I should get back to work."

"This whole city's falling apart," Tracy said. "That's what that story made me think about. When I was a kid I almost did imagine it turned into Camelot in the middle of the night. That wasn't really a joke."

"Well, I was just there in the middle of the night," Hober said. "It doesn't turn into Camelot."

"It was such a pit, you had to make up something just to put up with the place. Nobody does noble stuff around here anymore, for instance. Look at you. Henry had something wrong with his head and his father saved his life. Ricky had something wrong with his head and you slugged him one."

"Maybe that never happened to Henry," Hober said. "Maybe he made it all up."

"He didn't make up the hole in his head," Stu pointed out.

"He and Renee probably had a fight one time and she clobbered him with a frying pan."

"Don't be a jerk," Tracy said.

"Tracy," Hober told her, his forehead in his hands, "for God's sake. I haven't had any sleep for two days. I can't even remember how many cars I used since last night. I ended up with Raylene's, but DeLorea called me at five in the morning and wanted to know where his snowplow was. He was missing a snowplow. I couldn't remember what happened to it. I didn't even know which one he was talking about. Muencher borrowed the one I was driving. Maybe Muencher lost it somewhere."

"I think it was the old Canniman Brake Shoes plant," Tracy said after a minute. "When I was a kid, I thought it sort of looked like a castle. It had that turret on one end. And it was crenellated along the top."

Stu, who had been shaking a few uneaten French fries up and down in their paper packet, stood up and put his coat on. He had to get back to work. He said he was supposed to talk to Dave Beloschin, the Kroeber Tech principal, that afternoon. The snowmobile accident was certain to cause trouble with his job, he said, but he'd probably escape without being fired. It wasn't like D.W.I. and what had happened last year, when the local chapter of Mothers Against Drunk Driving had got Randy Ponzak, a history teacher at West High, drummed out of his job after the police had stopped him on a Saturday night. Ponzak had failed a blood test. "I don't think they've got any Mothers Against Kids on Snowmobiles," Stu said.

"Don't feel too bad," Tracy told him. "It could've been anybody's snowmobile. It just happened to be yours."

"That's right," Stu said to Hober. "I keep feeling like I should apologize to someone, but I can't apologize to you. You let him do it all the time."

"Yup."

"Well, it's the kind of thing guys do around here," Stu said after a minute. "Last night, when he didn't come back, I was thinking about that. It's snowing, the roads are bad, the visibility's awful, and this kid shows up, and he's hell on wheels—you couldn't trust this kid with a *doughnut.* Kid says, let me borrow your snowmobile, and if you're a normal guy around here, you say, 'Sure, let me start it up for you.' "

"You started it up for him?" Tracy asked.

"Fuckin' A. I still can't believe it."

"Well," Hober said. "If the little fucker keeps his butt out of trouble, he can use mine next winter. If he's learned his lesson. If he's figured out what a stop sign's for. The little fucker and I don't see this the same way you guys do."

"Listen to the way you talk about him!" Tracy yelled. "Little porker! Little fucker! You don't love your own son!"

"It's a nickname. It's a term of endearment."

"You don't even sound like you like him very much."

"I kind of like him right now, actually. I like the way he raises hell. I like the way he's tough. Last night he broke his wrist, he had a concussion, and I bashed him one on the way to the hospital, and he didn't moan or groan once. I'm starting to think he might turn out O.K."

"You guys are both awful."

"Well, you guys have both been in the dumps all fall," Hober said. "Maybe you better snap out of it. Stu's getting divorced, and you had your picture on the company bulletin board or something. That's really too bad, but it's time to stop feeling sorry for yourselves."

"And I don't like the way you run a crooked business," Tracy said. "Nancy Ortek told me what you did.

That stinks. She was really mad. What kind of muffler job is that?"

Hober crumpled up his coffee cup and put it through the swinging panel of the wastebasket next to their booth. "Listen," he said. "I run a business. I work six days a week. I help the city out when I have the flu. My kid gets in a mess in the middle of the night, I take him to the hospital. He has to go to the cops this afternoon, I'm taking him to the cops. Is that so bad? You make it sound like I'm some kind of bad person."

Stu gestured at the window. Ricky's chubby figure had appeared; he was getting out of Raylene's car. Raylene drove off—she and Tracy usually avoided each other. Beyond the shining windshields, the sun glinted off two of the fuel tanks, sending out bolts of light so searing that Hober winced and shut his eyes. "You see that little punk?" he said. "That little punk's going to medical school."

"Definitely," Stu said after a minute. "Right."

"You think I'm kidding? If he doesn't study, I'll whip his ass."

Tracy was still looking out the window. She seemed very tired. She said, "I think he's lighting a cigarette."